Distributed worldwide by Writer's Sanctum Publishing LTD

Cover art by: Writer's Sanctum Publishing

ISBN: 978-1-9998786-6-5

First Print: 23/07/2018

Visit our Website: www.writerssanctumpublishing.co.uk

To Lesley, as always,
and to Toby

A Parallel Life

by

Edmund Lester

Sunday September 3rd 2017, Hockley Heath, Solihull

Ben Williamson clicked the door of his CD player shut and pressed the play button. The opening bars of Billy Joel's Piano Man came from the speakers as he sat down in front of his computer and pressed the on button. It was a Sunday morning like all the other Sunday mornings in his life. He was working.

He looked through his to-do list. The first three items were all tax accounts; far too intense to break the day's duck. The fourth was perfect; annual returns for Smith Brothers, a small two man painting and decorating business in town. Past experience showed they were meticulous in their record keeping. Everything would be in order for him. It would be a simple task to complete the submission.

He hummed along to the music as he opened the previous year's filing to check where to start. This would be a simple matter. He should have it cleared up in little more than an hour. Behind him, in the main part of the house he heard Gilly start the vacuum cleaner. It was their bargain; *her suggestion*. She'd hoover the house, take care of the washing and prepare the Sunday lunch while he worked on his private clients. The rest of the housework they shared – unless they could get Naomi interested in helping, which wasn't often. He adored his daughter but wasn't blind to her idleness.

Smith Brothers had done well this year. Business was up, even subcontracting some work out, and their books were full. Dave Smith was even thinking of taking on an employee and had asked for advice on handling a payroll system.

It pleased him. They'd been one of his first private clients signing up back in 2007. They'd suffered through the financial crisis; really suffered. He'd been amazed they survived 2009. He scribbled a note on the To Do list so he'd remember to send them his PAYE documentation. He'd be happy to set it up for them but was going to advise them to look for someone who would work self-employed. It would make their lives easier.

He sipped his coffee and started sketching down the numbers long hand – his preferred method. He'd transcribe them to the computer once he was happy with the numbers. An hour later and he was done; accounts completed, ready to submit. The brothers would owe the tax man a little over three thousand pounds. They would be happy with that number. From the bank statements Dave had sent they had the money. Ben entered his password on the government website and got ready to complete the process. But that was as far as he got. Gilly flung open the door of his office. She looked scared stiff.

'Oh, thank God,' she exclaimed, falling back against the door of his office.

He got to his feet and made his way to her. She wrapped her arms around him the second he was in reach.
'What's up, love?' he asked.

'I thought you were dead.'

Ben couldn't believe the news report. He rewound it to make sure he'd not heard it wrong. He hadn't. He could see why Gilly had been so scared; the picture filling the top right of the screen behind the reporter was him, even down to the name under the image – Ben Williamson. And that wasn't the end of the things that linked them.

This morning, less than two hours ago, Ben Williamson was murdered on Drury Lane, Solihull. This man shared his name and they looked as though could be brothers, was killed outside the office were Ben himself worked.

Ben paused the TV; his double's picture full screen. This Ben Williamson had longer hair, styled in a way Ben had always wanted for his own but felt he could never do with all the corporate meetings he attended. He was more tanned too but the differences were minor. He could see why Gilly might have thought it was him. It was uncanny.

'I thought you must have headed into work to fetch some papers or something,' Gilly said, tears rolling down her cheeks again.

Ben reached out and hugged her to his chest. 'It's not me though, love. I'm still here. I'm okay.' He kissed her hair and rocked her gently. As he did so he stared at the man's face on screen. It was like looking in a mirror. He thought about reaching out to play the article again but stopped his hand halfway. It wouldn't be fair on Gilly. She was upset enough already. He clicked the off button instead.

He wondered what had happened to get his doppelganger killed. A paranoid thought went through his head. Was this man killed because of a simple misidentification? He imagined the scene. The killer had been waiting for him, Ben the accountant, and seeing this other Ben, this Ben 2, would have made the understandable error of thinking them the same person.

That person, male or female he wasn't going to judge, would have called out Ben or Mr. Williamson. His double would have turned thinking the person was after him. It was his name also. And as soon as the mystery assailant had seen his face he would have fired the gun.

A bullet would have flown quicker than anyone could react and killed Ben 2 instantly. Ben 2 could have been killed by mistake; in his place.

No, that didn't make sense. Who would want to kill an accountant? They weren't that important. And he'd never done anything outside his work life either to warrant such violence. He'd never cheated on his wife, so no jealous husbands to worry about. He had a limited social life, work occupied far too much of his time. And besides why would anyone go looking for him at the office on a Sunday?

Then it hit him; how close he had come to being the victim. If the killer had turned up at the same time on any day Monday to Friday looking for Ben 2, he or she would have found him on his way to work. It could be Ben whose death the news reporter was reporting. He felt a chill running up his spine.

Monday September 4th 2017, Solihull

Ben felt uneasy walking down Drury Lane towards the office. He kept looking around finding every face suspicious. He might have disagreed when Gilly suggested calling in sick but now he wished he had. It was only the thought Mr. Diamond and the Cookson account that stopped him. The deadline was growing ever closer and there was still a lot to finalise before the audit.

Halfway to his office the tent with the West Midlands Police logo on its side stopped him dead. He hadn't expected to see a police presence a day after the murder. When he'd seen the news report the previous day it hadn't featured the tent. In truth it was pretty vague about where on Drury Lane his double had been killed.

An old memory popped into his head. The shop he could no longer see used to be the jewellers where he'd bought Gilly's engagement ring. The two of them had headed there the day after he proposed. Gilly hadn't been sure he'd meant it until he paid the deposit.

He'd hated having to pay in instalments but just out of University he couldn't buy it outright. It had taken three months of instalments. But for all of those three months they had made their Saturday morning pilgrimage into town when she'd try the ring on for a few moments before handing it back. These were her practice sessions for when she would tell her friends and family. She hadn't wanted to announce it until she had the bling on her finger.

Robyn, the receptionist from the office tapped him on the shoulder interrupting his reverie. 'What's up Mr. W?' she said.

'I...' Ben paused a second. He looked at her. 'I died here yesterday, Robyn.'

'You what?' She looked upset at his statement. She couldn't have seen the news. Odd, in these days of social media he thought this kind of thing would have spread like wildfire.

'Sorry, I meant he died here; Ben Williamson.'

'But that's you, Ben. I don't get you.'

'I had a double, Robyn. And yesterday morning he was killed here; or rather there.' He pointed to the tent.

~*~

Robyn was the only one of his colleagues who hadn't heard of *his* death. Eagerly they filled him in on the details the later news reports, the ones he'd not watched, had added. His double had even made the national news, even if mainly as a "Do you remember…" type story.

Hearing that made him doubly glad he'd remembered to call Naomi at the boarding school, letting her know he was okay before any news could have filtered through to her. He'd offered to come and fetch her home. Naomi hesitated before answering. She must have been sorely tempted to rejoin them but had declined. She had only just returned to school and this was her exam year so she had better stay. He couldn't disagree with her.

Maxine, the company's lawyer recited all she could remember; with her memory that meant pretty much everything. Ben 2's life was much like his in many ways – to a point anyway. They'd both been raised in similar areas, less than two miles apart from the sound of things. Beoley, the village where Ben 2 spent his childhood was even the one his own parents had considered moving to before they'd chosen Wood End.

It explained why he'd never encountered his double before now. The two villages were in different counties. He'd grown up in Warwickshire; Ben 2 in Worcestershire. They'd have been in different school systems, with him heading to Stratford by train every morning and his double… Ben thought for a second. He wasn't sure where Ben 2 would have gone. He guessed it didn't matter.

The similarities were uncanny. They were both musical, playing in the school concert band before taking up guitar in their teens. But that's as far as it went for their parallel lives. After A-Levels Ben had let any thoughts of rock stardom die, He'd headed off to University and the real world.

Ben 2 though had stuck it out. His band, Domino Effect, had even signed to a record label, not one of the major labels but still impressive, put out a couple of albums in the nineties and even toured as support on several tours; including the USA. That was a life Ben would have killed for back when he was eighteen; far more exciting than accountancy.

Domino Effect had failed to make it big. The highest they managed in the charts was one week at number twenty three. The albums failed to dent the top hundred and the label didn't take up the option they had on a third.

Before Maxine could tell him anything more, Mr Diamond walked in. It surprised everyone. He never came into the office on a Monday – or a Friday for that matter, preferring to spend his weekends at his second home in the South of France. He could have only come back for one reason. He must have thought Ben was dead.

~*~

Mr. Diamond led Ben into his office and closed the door. Ben wasn't sure what he was going to say; some kind of pep talk maybe, an 'it wasn't you', 'there's no point moping about it' and 'far too much work to be done' kind of thing; that and, 'Try not to be a distraction to the others. They have their own work to do'. It wasn't that at all. The old man gave him the week off. 'Be with your family and get over the shock,' he'd said. When Ben started to protest, he had even volunteered to take care of the Cookson account himself.

Ben thought about declining the offer but the look on Mr. Diamond's face discouraged him. He nodded, and thanked him. It was a side of the senior partner Ben had never seen before. It almost seemed he cared.

His meeting over, Ben gathered his coat and briefcase. He opened it on his desk and started to pull together the files of the other accounts he was working on. Mr. Diamond stopped him. 'I don't want you working,' he said. 'We'll take care of all this.'

Ben nodded, left the files on his desk and reclosed his case. He said a few farewells, endured the endless procession of hugs and made his way to the office door. Mr. Diamond escorted him.

When they were alone and out of earshot the old man turned to him. 'I'm glad you're okay Ben,' he said. 'When my wife told me of your death yesterday – sorry I mean *his* death – I didn't know what to do. You are important to us all here, Ben.'

He held out his hand. Ben took it and shook it. 'Thank you, Sir.'

Mr. Diamond nodded. 'But don't let the others know I said any of this. I have a reputation to maintain. I don't want them to start thinking I'm soft.'

'I won't, Sir.'

Monday September 4th 2017, Hockley Heath, Solihull

Gilly's car was in the driveway when he got home. That was a good thing. So was her sister Ali's; not so good. Ben's relationship with Ali was abrasive to say the least, bordering on open warfare at times. Ali was overprotective of Gilly; never thinking anything, least of all Ben, good enough for her baby sister.

He tried to shake the negative thoughts from his head. At least her being there had meant Gilly hadn't had to be home alone after such a shock. Ben manoeuvred his car around Ali's, not an easy task with the angle she'd parked, and headed inside.

Gilly greeted him with a hug before he'd even closed the front door behind him. For the first time in all the years he'd known her Ali did the same as soon as Gilly had let go. No words had been spoken; none were needed.

When the hug eventually ended Gilly held onto his arm, not wanting to let go. Although not the most touchy-feely of people, today Ben accepted the contact and rather than the armchair he usually chose when they had company sat with Gilly on the main sofa; Ali having moved to allow them be together. Gilly pulled her lower legs up underneath her and moved as close to him as she could.

Few words were spoken that afternoon. No one could think of much to say. But despite this the afternoon passed quickly and it soon reached the time when they knew Ali had to go; her kids would be finishing school soon. Gilly unwrapped herself from Ben and hugged her sister goodbye. Ben found himself standing and hugging her too; a first. Today was a different day to normal that was for sure.

Once they were alone Ben suggested a movie might take their minds off everything. Gilly was reluctant until a mention of Love Actually, her favourite film, one of many she kept in the comfort viewing cupboard at the back of the lounge, changed her mind. He put the DVD into the player and poured them both a drink; a gin and tonic for Gilly, just the tonic for himself; he always avoided alcohol in stressful times, not wanting to view it as a crutch.

He returned to the sofa, again choosing it over his favourite armchair. Gilly leant in close as the opening scene started, wrapping an arm around him. She rested her head against his shoulder. As she settled in to watch the film Ben found his gaze moving away from the television screen towards the door to his office. Not out of any desire to work; there was far too much going through his head for him to concentrate on company accounts. He had this urge to research the man who died; find out who this man who was so much like him was.

It wasn't possible; not now anyway. But maybe when they went to bed he would get the chance. Gilly was a far heavier sleeper than him. His keeping the light on and using the iPad wasn't going to keep her awake. He could always look Ben 2 up after she was asleep. Yes, he would do that. Or so he thought. Later when they did head for bed Ben was actually the first to fall asleep, unconscious as soon as his head hit the pillow. And that's when the first dream came.

Tuesday September 5th, 2017, Hockley Heath, Solihull

Ben was surprised. Despite his plans for Ben 2 research being thwarted by his tiredness, he wasn't disappointed. There was actually a buzz to how he felt and this great tune, one he couldn't easily place, was going through his head. Normally earworms annoyed Ben and he relied on clearing tunes to get them to stop. But this was one tune he didn't want to let go of.

He sat down at their kitchen-diner with Gilly for breakfast. They didn't often get the chance to do this, not even at weekends. There was always too much to do. He should try being vicariously killed more often. Gilly raised the subject of how to pass their unexpected time together. Ben surprised himself, suggesting they make the most of it and the unusually warm late summer weather and go out for the day, a couple's day, something they'd rarely done since Naomi's birth.

The idea excited Gilly. She smiled for the first time since hearing of his double's death. They finished breakfast and were washing up the plates when the phone rang. Gilly dried her hands and walked across the kitchen to pick up the handset leaving Ben to finish clearing up. He listened in to the call, wondering who it might be.

After a few seconds, and a few yesses from Gilly, she covered the mouthpiece with a hand. 'It's for you,' she said. 'It's the police. They want to come here and talk to you.'

He felt confused why they might be calling. Were they thinking he might be involved in Ben 2's murder? He dried his own hands and joined his wife near the telephone. She passed the handset to him but stayed close enough to hear both sides of the conversation.

The officer, DI Jade Thomas, wanted to come over to discuss aspects of Ben 2's case. They'd learned of the coincidence canvassing the businesses around Drury Lane for information and wanted to just check out whether there was any connection between him and Ben 2.

Ben agreed and she suggested that afternoon, around one pm. Before he could say anything more DI Thomas was thanking him for his time and ending the call. Their planned day out wasn't going to happen. He felt disappointed. From the look on her face so was Gilly. He apologised to her. She tried to put a brave face on it, shrugging and saying there was always tomorrow. But Ben knew her too well.

At a loss of what to do now they were house bound, Ben suggested another movie session. Gilly agreed without much enthusiasm, even when he held up the box for Roadhouse. She'd had a thing for Patrick Swayze as long as he'd known her. She must have every film he made in her collection. How many times had he had to endure Dirty Dancing? Too many, that's how many.

He sat in front of the TV without paying any attention to the images or sounds coming from it. Too many things were swimming around in his head, now added to by the paranoid fear the detective had invoked in him. If she suspected a connection did that mean there was one? And did that mean Ben 2's killer might.

DI Thomas and her companion, a DS whose name Ben didn't catch, arrived exactly on time. Their punctuality surprised him. It soon became apparent this was part of who she was. Thomas was all business. There was no preamble. She had an efficient air about her and she put his mind at rest with regards one of the thoughts that had been plaguing him since her call earlier. They were not looking at him as a suspect in his double's death. The second thing though, she had no good news for him. As of yet they had not ascertained whether it was Ben 2 that was the target.

So there was still a possibility that his double had died in his place. There was still the possibility that the killer, having seen the wrong man was dead, might be thinking to find him and complete the job. She didn't think it likely. Ben 2's background and lifestyle made him by far the more likely target. 'After all,' she said. 'Who would want to murder an accountant?' She'd meant it in a jokey reassuring way. He appreciated her effort. It was just a shame it hadn't worked.

The rest of the interview was straightforward; a matter of dotting Is and crossing Ts. He knew they had to do it. It was too much of a coincidence for them to not follow it up. It was just a pity they hadn't arrived at his office yesterday so he could do all this there and not have to put Gilly through it.

Just before she left DI Thomas dropped her bombshell. She was posting two officers out front of their property just in case she was wrong about him being the target. She requested they only left the house when it was absolutely necessary for the rest of the week. She didn't have the resources to handle road-trip ride-alongs. It wasn't just today his plans for days out would come to nothing.

Wednesday September 6th 2017, Hockley Heath, Solihull

Gilly suggested she should cancel her hair appointment and lunch date with Ali. Ben told her not to. She should try to get back into her regular life as soon as possible, he'd said. When she argued that the police had requested they stay home he'd assured her he was sure it meant only him. She wasn't a target here. He wasn't either he added quickly to reassure her. He was sure of it. And in any case he could use the time to catch up on the work he missed out on doing Sunday.

She wasn't sure and was about to ring and cancel both, when he suggested he seek the advice of the police at the end of his drive. She thought about it for a moment or two then agreed. If the officers thought it was alright for her to go, she would.

He brewed up a flask of coffee and headed for the two men guarding him. They were initially dubious at his approach until he waved the thermos at them; fresh coffee his pass to friendly relations. The two men, Steve and Mike, on their first shift outside his home were both Sergeants. They were chatty; Mike even asking what property prices were out here. His wife was expecting their first and he thought the idea of raising a child in a semi-rural area appealed to him more than where he currently lived in King's Heath.

He stayed longer than he'd intended but it was important to be on good terms with the two men. If DI Thomas's worst case scenario came true he might need them to save his life. He would supply each pair with a fresh thermos early on in their shift. It didn't hurt to be civil and would only cost a few pounds for a new jar of coffee. He felt he could afford that.

When he returned inside he told her what the two officers had said. They were sure Gilly would be okay. Ben added a line about maybe getting Ali to come fetch Gilly. He implied the officers had said it but this was all him. He thought her too distracted to risk her driving. A few more words of how guilty he'd feel if she was cancelling his life for him and her last objection was dropped. She headed off to change and call Ali to get her to come over rather than meet in town.

Ben headed for his office, leaving the door open and not switching on the CD player. He didn't want to miss hearing Gilly come back downstairs. He would have most of the day to lock himself into his man cave and play his CDs.

The computer was still switched on. He couldn't have come back into the room since his wife burst in on Sunday. The Smith Brothers accounts were still on the left hand screen; on the right the web page on the revenue site read to transfer the accounts, although his login would have, without doubt, expired by now. He hadn't come back to complete the job on Sunday or since. He instinctively logged the page back in but didn't start the filing process. It would be his number one task when Gilly left.

He had a feeling though it would be the only work he did today. He couldn't get the idea of his double out of his head. He needed to know more about the man; who he was and how he died.

Before he could complete the thought he heard the horn of Ali's car outside. He walked across the lounge, down the hallway and opened the door to let her in.

'Who are the goons outside?' she asked by way of a greeting.

'They're my security detail,' he said with an air of mock self-importance in his voice. 'They're here to stop any would-be assailant getting in.'

'No shit,' she said. 'They stopped me before I could even get on the drive and wouldn't let me in until I proved I was who I said I was. Did you warn them I was coming?'

Ben nodded. 'I did.'

'Christ, what would it have been like if I'd turned up unannounced?'

Gilly came half-skipping, half-running down the stairs. 'Ali, thanks for coming.'

'No problem, baby-sis. I'm always here for you.' She turned her head towards Ben. 'Both of you,' she added.

'Thank you,' he mouthed back at her.

One final round of hugs and Ben was able to persuade his wife to go get on with her life and have a *girly day*, her description, with Ali.

Ben was impressed with his own strength of will. He'd headed straight from waving good bye to his wife to his office as planned and managed to keep to his earlier intention of completing the accounts he'd left undone. He almost hadn't managed it. He'd been tempted to save his work; come back to it later. Only that wouldn't be fair on Dave and Ian Smith. But it would be the last work he did that day. Accounts filed Ben was googling his doppelganger.

He clicked on the topmost link – Ben 2's own website benwilliamsonmusic.com. He was greeted by his own face staring back at him. He didn't know if he could ever get used to that. Maybe it was for the best that he'd not discovered him until only one of them remained alive.

He would not have been able to resist contacting Ben 2 – and that meeting would have been beyond freaky. That or, even worse, his double might not have wanted to meet. That would have driven Ben insane.

Once his initial surprise had faded he was able to look beyond the image dominating the page. He read down the menu on the left

- News
- About Ben
- Music / Downloads
- Gigs
- Gallery
- Domino Effect
- Contact
- Shop

He clicked on About Ben. He was here to find out more his double after all and began reading.

Ben Williamson was born in Solihull in 1967 but his family moved shortly afterwards and he grew up in Beoley in rural Worcestershire. His start in music was humble, the recorder at primary school, moving on to clarinet, saxophone and piano and playing in his secondary school band. He picked up his first guitar at age fourteen.

He formed the Domino Effect at Bromsgrove College with Thomas Paine on drums, Lewis Alford on bass, and George Scott on keyboards, occasional rhythm guitar and backing vocals. Ben played lead guitar, sang lead vocals, and was chief songwriter.

The Domino Effect played in public for the first time in July 1984 at the College where they met and quickly built up a strong local following, playing many gigs in the pubs and clubs of Birmingham, Redditch, Bromsgrove and Worcester over the next five years

A chance opening slot for established Birmingham band The Common Sense, when their official support act dropped out, lead to a record deal with Living Will records. Domino Effect (the leading "The" now no more) recorded their first album, Chain Reaction in autumn of 1990. First single, Rock Me, was rushed out for the Christmas market but failed to chart.

Early 1991 saw them head out on a world tour supporting legendary US rockers Pilgrim Boys, opening more than one hundred concerts across four continents, followed by a further road trip across Europe, with NWOBHM legend Titanic.

Second single, Riding all the Way to Hell, released to coincide the British leg, saw the band in the pop charts and an appearance on the Radio One Chart Show.

They recorded their second album Snowball Rolling Downhill in 1993 but it failed to chart. Realising that, in the age of grunge, their brand of glam metal was now sorely out of fashion the band called it quits in 1994. They have remained friends and reunite for gigs periodically.

Ben continued to write and perform music and moved into soundtrack work. His compositions have been used on more than two hundred commercials and a dozen television series.

Ben has also released several solo albums on his own Cascading Records label and performs more than fifty solo gigs each year all across England, Wales and Scotland in addition to his Domino Effect reunions.

For more details on where you might see Ben live click the Gigs button on the left.

It was a fairly standard bio. Ben was a keen music fan and had read hundreds of similar write ups. What surprised him about it was the fact the similarities between the two of them grew more all the time.

Reading it in greater detail just raised more parallels between their early lives. Was this what his life was like if he'd decided to make a go of it with his own band? Would he too have had a brief taste of the rock life to see it denied him in full glory? Would he have been happy with that?

Ben clicked on the Music button. There were links to five videos of Domino Effect songs on the left and of Ben 2's solo work on the right. The images of Ben 2 in his band days were scary – all glammed up with big hair and eyeliner. Ben chose the first of the links, the hit single mentioned in the bio, Riding all the Way to Hell and maximised the video.

It was everything Ben would expect of Glam Metal – think of Mötley Crüe or Poison and you pretty much had the look down; the music too if he was honest. It was nothing special; all crunchy chords and sub-Aerosmith riffs. But in was in the lyrics that they had truly excelled – only the wrong way. They were terrible, over the top puerile and embarrassing. Ben hoped no one that knew him found this video and thought it was him at age 23 cavorting in the tight leather trousers and ripped tee-shirt.

He closed the video and returned to Google. The next entry on the list was Ben 2's entry on Wikipedia. He clicked on it hoping to find out more. It didn't help. What was held on the Wikipedia page was a word for word copy of the bio he'd just read on Ben 2's page followed by a discography. He hadn't checked the one on the official website but he would put money on the two being identical. This wiki page was in all likelihood the work of his double, or maybe his double's webmaster; all part of the service.

Several other websites later Ben hadn't found out anything more about his namesake. For a musician there wasn't much on the net about him. Irritated by his lack of progress Ben clicked on the news option on Google. Here were dozens of entries, all about his death. He read one or two of them until decided he'd read all there was. All the time he was humming Riding all the Way to Hell under his breath. For all the fact he thought it worthy of being a flop as a single he couldn't get the tune out of his mind.

He opened YouTube and typed in Domino Effect. The list of links that greeted him was familiar. It was like the Wikipedia feeling all over again. He opened a second copy of IE and retrieved Ben 2's website. He put the two side by side and compared the two lists. The same five as appeared on both sites. The only difference between the two pages was YouTube added further suggestions to the page, all by other but comparable late eighties glam metal bands.

What surprised him was the lack of any links on YouTube to Ben's solo work. He had expected

YouTube's software would have returned them as related videos but they were not there. He typed in Ben 2's name, his name, into the Search box and clicked on the looking glass icon.

He knew what would be returned before the browser had completed loading the page. There they were; the same five Ben Williamson solo videos that were featured on Ben 2's site; and once again in the same order. This time the additional entries on the list YouTube returned contained a name that Ben recognised. He re-opened Ben 2's bio page. There it was – George Scott, Domino Effect's keyboard player had tried his own hand at solo recording. None of the others featured though. They must have left the music industry, re-joining the real world.

Ben was irritated. He needed to know more about his double. He guessed it would take a lot more work to find out anything more. He clicked on the second video link on YouTube for Domino Effect. He may as well have music to listen to while he searched the net.

Thursday September 7th 2017, Hockley Heath, Solihull

The early hours of the next morning saw the first of the dreams Ben would remember on waking. In fact it woke him up. It was the most vivid dream Ben had ever experienced and, on waking, he remembered every single detail. Its content didn't come as a shock. After a day of investigating his double it was inevitable he would dream about being him. He would have been more surprised if his dreams had not featured Ben 2.

The dream had opened with him, as Ben 2, waiting in the wings behind the stage curtain. Out front he could hear the announcer beginning to stir up the crowd. Seconds later, just before stepping out from his hiding place and into the spotlights, a short stocky man, Ben knew to be one of Domino Effect's roadies handed him a Flame Burst Les Paul guitar. It was beautiful to look at and, he knew, beautiful to play.

As the disembodied voice of the announcer screamed out Domino Effect he ran out onto the stage and let rip with a power chord. Without any timewasting he launched into the band's opening song, To the Devil a Daughter. This was the first odd thing about the dream when he ran it back through his now awake mind.

He knew it to be a Domino Effect track, the title was on the album listing on Ben 2's website but he'd not been able to find any video or audio files for it, yet his subconscious mind had reproduced it for him in full, guitar solo and all.

He tried to logic out what had happened. He couldn't exactly be channelling his dead double's spirit, could he? This was just his mind inventing things, making it up based the sound and lyrics he'd listened to on the net. Was it much of a stretch to do that? Ben 2's range was not exactly the greatest in the world. At least not from the five songs Ben had heard.

His picking of that song even made sense to him. The title was an obvious lift from the Dennis Wheatley novel and Hammer Film of the 1970s. Ben had had a crush on Nastassja Kinski when he was a teenager. He presumed his double had too. For once he didn't find the coincidence spooky. As Ben 2 was the same age as him, he would have been suspicious if Ben 2's teenage self hadn't shared his opinion about the actress physical charms.

That must be it. His subconscious was filling in the blanks, creating its own version of a Domino Effect song. What else made sense? The only problem was Ben knew it wasn't true. And he knew one other thing. The song wanted to be played. It wasn't going to let him sleep.

Ben looked at the bedside clock. Its luminous hands indicated it was 3:40am. He'd been asleep less than four hours but that would be it for this night. He sat up on the edge of the bed and turned on his sidelight and reached for the notepad and pen he kept by the side of the bed, scribbling down...

> *Couldn't sleep*
> *Didn't want to wake you*
> *Am in the basement.*

He placed the note on his side of the bed and tiptoed from the room. He thought about grabbing a bathrobe before he headed downstairs. He dismissed it. The idea of walking near-naked through the house was unusual to him but it was better than being wrapped in terry towelling a stifling late summer night.

When he'd first seen the house one of the things that had attracted him to it was the basement. He'd had dreams of playing music again, even going as far as having it soundproofed to spare the rest of the family his out of tune efforts.

It hadn't materialised of course, other than a jam session or two with the one member of his old band he was still in touch with. They talked about trying to track down the others and seeing if they still had it but neither did anything about it. Over the years he'd come down here less and less and it was little more than a storage room now.

His instruments were still here though including the Les Paul. It wasn't an early Flame Burst model like in his dream. This model was a 2000 one in bright red with white trim, he'd picked up second hand during the early days of his midlife crisis; the MX5 sports car he'd driven for two years around the same time being the most conspicuous. Naomi's move to boarding school and the fees that meant quickly ended such insanity – just in time he'd realised. He had been considering buying a Harley-Davidson and he couldn't even ride a motorbike. Gilly would have gone nuts about that.

He pulled the Les Paul from its stand. The thick layer of dust on it shocked him. Had it been that long since he'd last played it? He searched in the supplies cupboard along the back wall for the cleaning cloths he would need to get it ready to play.

~*~

Ben switched on the amplifier; time to test the soundproofing…well, you can't play an instrument like this without electrical help. It just wasn't right.

He sat down on the chair in front of the amp, balanced the guitar on his right knee and formed the power chord he'd played in his dream. His fingers just fitted into the shape easily. It felt so natural. He strummed the plectrum across the top three strings. It sounded superb, chunky and heavy with just the right amount of fuzz. He glanced down at the pedals. He had no memory of changing the settings on his effects board. When he used to play, he never went for this sound. He must have just done it without thinking.

Something was not quite right though, and he knew just what it was. Music like this wasn't meant to be played sitting down. He needed a guitar strap. He dropped the guitar back onto its stand and rummaged through the various boxes.

Satisfied the strap was fastened securely he stood and allowed the weight to settle on his shoulders. That felt better, even given the slight chafing of the leather on his bare skin. He let the guitar just hang for a few seconds enjoying the experience. Why hadn't he done this before?

He wasn't here just to pose with the instrument though. He needed to play. He wrapped his left hand around the neck, reformed the opening chord then brought his right hand down across the strings. This time though, he didn't pause after just one chord. He carried on playing the guitar line from To the Devil a Daughter, and when the introduction reached his conclusion he started singing the verse.

He reached the end of the song and held the final note for an eternity. The best thing about a Les Paul was its sustain. Hold down any string at the higher end and it just lasted and lasted.

As the note faded away, Ben heard a clapping from behind him. All of a sudden he was self-conscious. He was aware of just how ridiculous a site he must have been; a near-naked, pudgy, pale skinned middle aged man playing guitar. He felt embarrassed even though it was only Gilly that had seen him.

~*~

Back in the lounge and thankfully covered in a tee-shirt Ben felt more comfortable. He drank a mouthful of coffee. 'I didn't know you could play like that.' Gilly said in between blowing on her still too warm drink, a much more sensible given the hour, caffeine-free fruit tea.

'Neither did I.' Ben didn't think he'd ever played that well in his life and after so many years of not practicing it was weird; troublingly so.

'Was that one of your band's old songs?'

'No,' Ben said. He took another sip of his coffee hesitant to answer her question more fully. Why hadn't he thought to add a slug of whisky to his mug? 'It's one of his,' He admitted, not needing to say any more, Gilly knew exactly who he meant.

'So how can you play it so well?' she asked. 'You said earlier you were unaware of your double's music until you found him on the internet.'

'And I was telling the truth. I never heard them back in the day; as far as I know. I definitely never saw them live. I checked through their tour dates in case I'd caught them supporting Maiden or someone like that but no. As far as I am aware I never heard any of his songs until earlier today.'

'So did you learn that from just a couple of listens?'

'No,' he said. He couldn't have. He never had the knack of hearing a piece of music and being able to play it back.

'You must have done. There's no other explanation.'

'I'm sorry, Gilly, but you're wrong. It just isn't possible.'

'It has to be though. There's no other explanation. Why would you deny it?'

'Because the track I played isn't one of the ones I found online. I only know of it from the track listing of their albums on Ben's website.'

'So how did you just play it?' she asked. Ben could see she was scared. He didn't blame here; this was freaky stuff.

'I guess it isn't really their song,' he said trying to reassure her. 'It can't be.'

'What was it then?'

'I don't know. Maybe my subconscious just created it all from the various parts I'd heard earlier. The lyrics could have come from the film. I watched it over and over when I was a kid.'

'You did?' Gilly asked. She was still a little suspicious. 'I suppose that Kinski woman was naked in it.'

'She might have been,' Ben admitted in a mock embarrassed voice. He hoped if he played it up Gilly might buy this as the origin of his night time performance.

'I never did understand your half of the species.'

'I guess we never lose the teenage boy.' He tapped his temple. 'Some of it must still be in here forever.'

'More like somewhere else,' Gilly replied, her eye-line moving lower. 'Well if it causes you to play guitar like that you should let your teenage self out from time to time. That was great.'

~*~

Despite Ben's certainty of remaining awake he was asleep again seconds after returning to bed. The next time he woke it wasn't a dream of Domino Effect that ended his sleep; the phone on the bedside table rang.

Still half-asleep he reached across, almost fumbling it onto the floor. 'Good morning,' he said when he finally got the handset to his ear. DI Jade Thomas greeted him in returning. Hearing her voice caused him to pull himself closer to vertical. 'How can I help you, Inspector?' he asked.

Gilly was now awake too. She listened in to the conversation although with it being as one sided in the favour of the police detective as it was she found the experience frustrating. She decided it was better to wait, slipped out of bed and headed for the bathroom.

When she returned Ben was in the middle of saying his goodbyes. 'What was all that about?' she asked.

'They've arrested someone for his murder,' Ben said. His voice sounded hollow.

'That's good isn't it?' Gilly asked.

'I guess so,' he said. He wasn't so sure. What the DI had said deflated him.

Gilly shuffled herself across on the bed and wrapped her arms around her husband's shoulders. 'Did they tell you any of the details?' she asked.

'It was one of his band mates, the keyboard player George Scott. He's admitted it; all over a dispute over song writing credits… and money I guess.'

'Well that's a good thing for us, isn't it?'

Ben stared at her; a puzzled look on his face. 'What do you mean?'

'Well, if your namesake was the intended target then no one is threatening you. You can get your life back to normal.'

'I guess so,' he said.

'What's the matter? I thought this would make you happy.'

Ben shrugged. 'It just seems such a mundane way for his life to end; an argument over money.'

'Was it a large sum?' Gilly asked.

'I wouldn't have thought so,' Ben replied. 'The band never got the sales they deserved. I can't see how they'd be earning the kinds of money that would make someone kill. It just seems senseless.'

'You think they deserved to be bigger?'

Ben looked shocked. His face looked mortified. 'Of course they did? Didn't you hear their music?'

'Only what you played me yesterday in your office. It didn't sound that inspiring to me, to be honest.'

He pulled away from her. 'How can you say that? Ben put his heart and soul into those songs.'

'But they sound like countless other bands to me.' She regretted her words as soon as they were out of her mouth. Ben's face hardened. He was angry; over something as stupid as a band he'd never even heard of before this week. 'I'm sorry,' she said. 'I didn't mean anything by that.'

She heard a knocking on the front door downstairs. The combination of tense atmosphere in the bedroom and the sudden noise made her squeal. 'Who's that?' she asked.

'It'll be one of the policemen from out front,' Ben replied. 'DI Thomas told me they were pulling them out now they have confirmed I wasn't the target.' He got to his feet and reached for his bathrobe. 'I'll go say goodbye to them.' He walked out of the room without another word or a backwards glance.

~*~

When he got back Ben declined Gilly's suggestion a day out to unwind, claiming the need to get back to work. Having had his Sunday disrupted he was behind schedule on his private work. A day or two concentrating on it and he'd have everything finished. It wasn't the real reason though. Her words had angered him and spending the day with her was the last thing he wanted to do. She sensed this too.

Gilly requested they at least eat breakfast together before he locked himself in his office. It took effort but he agreed. He even managed to smile, almost meaning it, when she suggested cooking scrambled eggs and bacon. The coy grin when he asked if she could add some fried mushrooms seemed to settle her nerves somewhat.

Hopefully she would think she was just being over-sensitive, not unusual for her. She settled back into the pillow and reached for her novel as he headed for the shower. All seems good, Ben thought.

Ben tried to act like his normal self throughout the meal, even chastising her playfully over her habit of checking the news on her iPhone as they ate. Gilly was buying it. She was calmer by meal's end, although obviously sad Ben was heading to his office. She'd wanted those days out they'd discussed but a quick mention of the due date for Naomi's school fees ended all protests.

Ben was relieved when he closed the door and was alone again. How could she have been so insensitive? Domino Effect was a great band. It was just bad timing and an inept record company that kept them from attaining the heights Iron Maiden, Metallica and the other top Heavy Metal bands reached. In a perfect world they would have rivalled the Rolling Stones.

Ben turned on his computer and spread a couple of his clients' files across the right hand side of his desk. He didn't think working on them was likely today but wanted it to look right in case Gilly interrupted him. There was only one thing on his mind today; Ben Williamson the rock star.

Yesterday's internet searches had return little but maybe he'd just gone about it wrong; given up too easily. There was more out there. He just had to find it. Maybe Google was hiding it. He would repeat his searches on Yahoo, Bing any other search engine he could find; he wasn't going to stop until he had found something more.

He opened Internet Explorer and browsed to YouTube; he may as well be able to listen to their music as he worked.

~*~

An hour, and dozens of pages of search results, later Ben had turned up nothing he didn't already know. He couldn't understand it. There must be more out there. He googled the other members of Domino Effect; everyone was on the internet these days. Naomi goggled herself all the time; it had worried Ben when she showed him how much of her life was there for all to see. He'd even asked her to cut back on her posting but she'd just laughed at him and told him to get out of the cave he was living in.

Shortly after that conversation Ben had been tempted to google himself. Something stopped him; it just felt too narcissistic. He wished he'd done it now. He would have found his doppelganger while he still lived. He could have met the man. He shook his head to rid himself of the regret; it wouldn't help now. Dwelling on it would stop him finding out more about Ben 2. He returned to his search.

Ben 2's fellow band members were digital ghosts; the only mentions on pages about Domino Effect. There was not even a local parish newsletter reporting on a local 'celebrity' opening a church fete – the kind of thing he imagined failed rock stars would do for attention.

A revelation struck him. The internet is mostly there trying to sell you things. Maybe for once it would have something he wanted to buy. He clicked on the Shopping menu button. Why hadn't he thought of that earlier? He might be able to buy the Domino Effect records. Google returned pitifully few entries, mainly ebay listings.

He clicked on the first two expectantly to find both expired. Damn! He banged a hand on the desk. A stupid reaction, he knew; the noise might cause Gilly to come in. He readied himself for her entry; rubbing hard on one knee faking an accidental impact with the desk leg turning round. A minute later he returned to his searching, satisfied he would not be interrupted.

He typed in the URL for ebay, someone might have added a new listing, and entered Domino Effect into the search box. A page showing fifty results flashed up in front of him. At the top of the screen it announced there were 1,307 listings that matched his search. He felt his heart speed up with excitement.

It didn't last. Most of the listings were for canvas prints of Vespa scooters, Doctor Who novels, various other books sharing the title, other bands' CDs where the album name was Domino Effect and Max Factor eyeshadow. He scrolled down the page without finding what he wanted – no, what he needed. The fifty listings on page one were a bust.

The second page was much like the first; the third and fourth likewise. He was beginning to grow despondent. He was just about to give up when the tenth page held what he was looking for. On screen was a thumbnail image showing both album covers, side by side. He clicked on the link before even registering any details. When the item page loaded he was shocked to see the price. The seller, vintage-vinyl-dreams had the two LPs on a 'Buy It Now' for £125. Ben was staggered by the amount.

He wanted those records. No he needed them. But could he justify spending £125 on two old records. He tried to resist clicking the button but it was hopeless. Even for the over the top sum the seller wanted, he had no choice. He entered his login details and confirmed the purchase. They were his.

He read a little more about the seller, an independent record shop in Southampton. Ben hadn't thought many of them still survived. Ben could go and collect the records. He glanced at the wall clock. It was eleven thirty. Could he get there today? He browsed to the AA Route Planner. The trip would take two hours ten minutes. The records could be in his hands before two o' clock.

He was out of his seat and halfway to the door when something Naomi had told him months before held him back. You can rip YouTube songs to MP3s. He could drive there and back listening to Domino Effect. It might only be five songs but it was better than nothing. He fished in his desk for a memory stick.

As the last song ripped he gathered a number of client files, bundling them into his briefcase; enough to stop Gilly wanting to come with him. This was his time. He wasn't going to share.

Thursday September 7th 2017, Southampton

Ben sat in the driver's seat staring at his purchases. He was ecstatic. This trip was one of the best decisions he'd ever made. Not only had Vintage Vinyl Dreams had the two LPs but Dom, the owner had found in stock, a copy of Domino Effect's debut single, Rock Me and an old tour tee-shirt.

That last item was a real Holy Grail item. He'd bought it despite it being a size too small for him. He could lose weight. That would be good. He'd be the same build as Ben 2 then.

But there was more to it than just the items. He felt he fitted in. Dom had understood his need; in the way that it was obvious already that Gilly never would. He was a collector. Their tastes may differ, Dom professing a love for reggae, but at heart it was the same. And Dom understood Ben needed more. He handed Ben a pamphlet listing other independent and second hand record dealers across the South of England as he left.

The closest to Solihull was an hour's drive but it didn't matter. For the right item he would drive to Moscow and back. Each of these businesses would receive an email from him as soon as he was home. Maybe one of them would have more Domino Effect items. He had outlets other than just ebay. Maybe there might be baseball caps, scarves or badges. He tried to remember what merchandise stands at gigs used to be like back in the early nineties.

His recollections showed them to be far less materialistic than today. Bands back then used to have tee shirts, button badges, programmes and not that much else; apart from maybe Kiss. They've always appeared on everything. And with Domino Effect being the support bands on most of their live work it would be more limited than headline acts. There might not be that much out there. Whatever there was though, Ben knew he needed it all.

As he put the LPs back into the record bag he noticed something in the acknowledgements. Domino Effect would like to thank Gibson Guitars, Yamaha Keyboards, and Premier Drums and Zildjian Cymbals and their management company, the Hit Talent Agency.

It hadn't occurred to Ben to search for the band's agent. They might even be still going. He pulled the LPs out again and checked the liner notes; on the inner sleeve as well as the outer sleeve. No address was listed. He needed to find out who they were and where they were. They might be able to tell him what he needed to know.

He started the car and reversed it out of the parking space. As the engine fired the car's music system auto started. Rock Me, the single he'd just bought on 7", blasted out of the speakers. Ben sang along with his double as he began his drive back to the Midlands.

Friday September 8th 2017, Hockley Heath, Solihull

The Hit Talent Agency was no more, folding in the late nineties. It hadn't survived Domino Effect by long. For a while Ben feared it was another dead end until he found an interview with John Reuben, the agent representing Domino Effect for them. He was still in the business, working for another agency. Yell.com provided the phone number and as he sat listening to the ring tone Ben felt progress was about to be made.

'Hello, Premium Talent; how may I help you?' came the receptionist's voice.

'Can I speak with Mr. John Reuben, please?'

'I'll just check whether he's in the office today, Sir.' A clicking sound and the hold music started; uninspiring dance music —one of the agency's hopefuls? If it was, the poor audio wasn't doing the music any favours. Not that Ben thought it had anything to warrant a fuller listen.

'Mr. Reuben is available, Sir,' the voice said, interrupting the inane drumbeat. 'Can I ask to what it is referring?'

Ben had no idea what to say. He'd not thought this far ahead. Should he just tell the truth or was a lie the better option? The truth. Or at least a version of it. 'I'm looking for the agent representing Ben Williamson and Domino Effect.'

'Thank you, Sir,' came the chirpy response. 'Putting you through.'

Thankfully the hold music didn't start up again. He was straight through. 'John Reuben here, before we start can I ask which publication you work for?'

'I'm sorry,' Ben replied. 'Which what?'

'Newspaper or magazine,' Reuben replied. Ben could hear a slight note of annoyance in his voice.

'I don't work for a paper,' Ben admitted.

'Website then? Or blog – just need a name for my file.'

'I don't work for a website either.'

'Television or radio?'

'No, nothing like that, Mr. Reuben.'

'Who are you then?' Reuben demanded.

'I'm Ben Williamson,' Ben said without thinking.

Reuben sighed. 'So this is a fucking joke then. Look Mister, I don't have time for prank calls. Don't try persuading me you're my client back from the dead. I'm a busy man. I have dozens more journos trying to get hold of me; people worth me talking to.'

Reuben's words contained a lot of bravado; a lot of bragging. But something sounded hollow. Ben did something he'd not have done a week before. He challenged him. 'Do you really, Mr. Reuben. If that was the case wouldn't your secretary have verified who I was before putting me through?'

There was a hesitation on the other end of the line. 'She's new,' Reuben said, 'and needs training.' Another hesitation. 'Anyway, I'm hanging up. I have better things to do.'

'I don't believe you,' Ben said.

'You what?'

'I don't believe you.'

'Look, you annoying fuck. I don't care what you believe or don't believe. I don't have time for your shit.'

The line went dead. Ben was angry. He'd called Reuben with nothing but good intentions only to be blown off without him even finding out what Ben wanted. If Reuben had been like this when Domino Effect were trying to make a go of it they'd never have had a chance. Agents were supposed to help their clients, not hinder them.

Ben stared at the phone unsure of what to do. No, that was untrue. He knew exactly what he wanted to do. He wanted to go beat the shit out of the man who hung up.

He'd never do it though. Not for any moral reason; if he killed Reuben it would be self-defeating. Reuben must know a lot about Ben 2 and alive there was a chance Ben could persuade him to talk; dead not so much. Maybe just a little torture…

Friday September 8th 2017, Warwick

Ben was surprised to find Reuben based in Warwick; just a short drive away. He'd always thought these companies would be based in London. It made him happy; he could drive down and confront the man. Face to face there would be no way he could deny that he was telling the truth.

Ben opened the door of the agency and walked over to the empty reception window. He pressed the buzzer and waited. The same inane dance music he'd heard on the phone was playing in the small lobby area. After five minutes alone with it he was contemplating ripping the two speakers from their fittings to stop the racket.

They were saved when the window behind him slid open. 'Good morning, Sir, how may I…'

The receptionist never finished the question. When Ben turned round to face her she screamed. Ben looked around trying to see what had caused her reaction. There was no one else here. What could have…? It hit him. From her point of view he was dead. But before he could tell her she was not imagining things and that he was not a ghost she'd run off screaming.

He stood immobile not knowing what he should do. Should he stay? His mind flashed images of someone rushing him from the side door armed with a baseball bat. In this small lobby space he would have no chance of avoiding attack. He glanced back at the exit. Maybe a hasty retreat would be for the best.

He took the first step and stopped. That was exactly what he'd done his entire life. It was why he'd quit his high school band and headed to university. His whole life had been the safe option. His double hadn't and Ben wanted to be more like him. Ben 2 had done what he wanted and though it hadn't turned out as hoped, as he'd deserved, he'd not quit. Until the day of his death Ben 2 made his living from music – better than filling in small business tax returns.

Ben stayed where he was and waited for whatever fate came his way.

A minute or so later another face peered around the reception window; this time it was a man. He stared at Ben. Ben stared straight back. The man, rather shorter than him and with hair heading rapidly towards comb-over seemed unsure of what to do but at least he wasn't screaming.

'Hello,' he said, albeit hesitantly.

Ben recognised his voice immediate as belonging to John Reuben. 'Mr. Reuben, my name is Ben Williamson. We spoke earlier.'

'We did?'

'Yes, and you slammed the phone down on me.'

'I did?'

'Yes,' Ben confirmed. 'Now are you going to let me in or do we have to talk through a wall?' He pointed a finger over towards the door.

'I…' Reuben was confused. He continued staring at Ben. 'Give me a minute.' And with that he was gone. Ben was alone again.

~*~

Eventually the door opened only it wasn't Reuben that appeared from behind it. This man was much younger and much larger; *much larger*. Ben guessed maybe 6'7" or 6'8" – scary tall; no doubt the agency's security guy, or the guy they'd call on to do security for their clients.

Had they'd sent this guy out to intimidate him? Up until a week ago it would have worked. But since finding out about his double and hearing his music, Ben was a completely different man. He unfolded his arms, tucking each thumb into a belt loop on his jeans and stood his ground.

'So Reuben's sent you out to check me out?' he said. 'Too scared to come talk to me in person?'

'That's pretty much the gist of it,' the giant in front of him admitted. 'I'm to make sure there's nothing funny going on. And to make sure you're real.'

'Real?' Ben replied. He didn't try to hide the annoyance. 'Do they think I'm a ghost or something?'

'Well, being honest, Mister, we were told you were dead; murdered. Most people don't get up after that. Mr. Reuben just asked me to find out what you were.'

'I'm an accountant,' Ben replied flippantly.

The big man ignored him, stepped closer and gingerly reached across to prod Ben's shoulder. Ben didn't flinch. 'So are you satisfied I'm not a ghost?'

'I guess. Unless… Can ghosts be solid?' he asked.

'How would I know?' Ben said snippily. 'I don't even believe in them.'

The security man pondered it for a few seconds. 'Okay, well if you're not a ghost I need to check that nothing else funny is going on.'

'Like what?'

'Well Mr. Reuben still thinks it might be a scam. I've got to check whether you're wearing a mask or something to make you look like Ben; and whether you're wearing a wire.'

'A wire? What does he think this is? Some kind of spy thriller?'

'Sorry man, I didn't set the rules. You don't pass I'm to throw you out the door.'

'Do what you need to do,' he said. He unhooked his thumbs and held his arms out wide.

The big man moved closer and placed his hands on Ben's face. He prodded and pulled at his cheeks and ears. Satisfied with his head he patted him down looking for some kind of electronic device. 'Would you put the contents of your pockets on the table?'

Ben sighed, stepped back and emptied his pockets. He watched the big guy examine his ID, looking back and forth between his driving licence and face before turning it over; checking if it was a fake, Ben guessed.

He handed it back to Ben and moved back to the window, tapping on the glass three times. 'He's real, boss.'

~*~

Reuben sat across the desk from him, still staring. There was a question, many questions, he wanted answers for. Ben wasn't going to make it easy for him, despite his own need for information. He'd been put through enough already by this guy.

'So you're Ben Williamson?' Reuben asked.

'You know I am, Mr. Reuben. Your goon checked me out, didn't he?'

'Ben Williamson is dead. You're not him. Did you change your name to cash in on your lookalike appearance? If you did, joke was on you when Domino Effect failed to make it big.' He laughed.

'No, Mr. Reuben. I'd never heard of Domino Effect or my double before Sunday.'

Ben reached to the edge of the desk to retrieve his glass of water. Reuben flinched at the sudden movement. Ben enjoyed the man's fear. He'd never been the type to elicit such a reaction from anyone. As a kid he'd been the one who suffered at the hands of others, not the other way around.

'So why are you here?' Reuben asked.

'I want to know more about him, about Ben Williamson, the rock star.'

'Rock Star?' Reuben scoffed. The fear left him in an instant. The sudden change unsettled Ben. Reuben was a schemer. It was obvious just looking at him. He must be working out how he could bend this situation to his benefit and it seemed he'd just figured it out. 'Ben my boy… I can call you Ben can't I?' he asked. Ben nodded. Reuben continued, 'I think I might be able to help. But, if I do, would you be willing to do something for me?'

Here it comes. 'What do you want me to do?'

'Nothing to arduous I assure you; nothing illegal.'

'But immoral I bet,' Ben countered.

'Aren't Morality and immorality just a matter of perspective,' Reuben said. 'Give me a minute. Hear me out. Then I'll answer all your questions.'

Ben appreciated the man for not trying to pretend his attentions were honourable. 'I guess it wouldn't hurt to hear what you want. Listening to something doesn't mean it's going to happen.'

'Oh, my boy, I think you'll like this.'

Saturday September 9th 2017, Hockley Heath, Solihull

Sleep wasn't easy coming; too much swimming round his head. By four am Ben stopped trying. Reuben had floored him with everything he'd said. The first and biggest revelation was that Domino Effect had recorded a new album before Ben 2's death. They'd listed themselves on a crowdfunding site and received enough donations to book studio space for a week. The album was done. All that remained was mastering and it was off to the record label, in time for the Christmas market.

Studio time to shoot videos for the singles to support the album was booked. All was going perfectly until George Scott got pissed off over a denied co-writing credit no one but Scott thought he deserved. He and Ben 2 had fallen out in a big way, fists flying. Both men left the rehearsal session with cuts and bruises; Ben 2's left eye swollen shut. The video shoot was a bust. Reuben sent them home to heal and calm down.

Only Scott hadn't calmed down and killed Ben 2 before the rescheduled video shoot. Without videos it would be a lot harder to promote the release, even given all the free publicity of Ben 2's murder by his keyboard player.

That is it would have been except for Ben giving him a "great idea". Ben could stand in for his double.

In any other circumstances Ben would have found it outrageous; no, worse downright dishonest. Stand in for his double for the videos? Take Ben 2's place and pretend they were shot before he died?

Ben was shocked. He wasn't worthy of taking his double's place. He tried to tell Reuben but the man wouldn't listen; presuming he was just arguing he couldn't play guitar. He reassured Ben they'd just film it from all the right angles and edit it so it looked right – no one would know he wasn't playing.

Without thinking Ben admitted 'But I can play... Just...' He'd intended to explain having a little skill on the guitar meant he knew it wouldn't work but Reuben didn't let him get to the explanation. Hearing Ben could play the guitar just told Reuben it was meant to be. He moved on to more mundane things; money. Ben would get paid. No doubt this was the winning argument in his usual dealings.

The money was of secondary interest. He just wanted to hear the music. No, more than that; he needed to hear it. Waiting until the album was released was unbearable. If he agreed to Reuben's request he could maybe get an advanced copy; so he could learn the songs for the video shoot of course. He suggested it. Reuben just smiled, 'Sure. We can do that.'

~*~

As if he didn't have enough to think about with his upcoming video shoot, Reuben dropped in one final revelation as he drew up a contract to cover payment for his appearances, described as "accountancy services" to keep the whole thing a secret. Ben's girlfriend had contacted an auction house. Everything Ben 2 owned would be going up for sale; and soon.

It was distasteful so soon after Ben 2's death – even Reuben for all his money grabbing nature found it so – but Ben 2's latest girlfriend Ingrid, an American junkie, must feel her gravy train was leaving the station and desperately wanted to grab whatever she could get. Reuben expected her to buy enough blow or smack to fly her way to the devil.

Ben was torn. It was tawdry; Ben's genius being exchanged for bags of white powder. But he did feel a thrill at the thought of being able to own some of his double's possessions.

Reuben gave him the details of the solicitor dealing with Ben 2's account and the auction house handling the sale. Ben 2's girlfriend wanted it to happen before the end of the month. Reuben thought that unlikely in such a timeframe, but it wouldn't be long after.

Everything was up for sale, his house, its contents, Ben's guitars and other instruments, everything. There was one thing in particular that Ben wanted. He wanted the vintage Flame Burst Les Paul guitar. He had to have it.

In place of sleep Ben spent the pre-dawn hours searching the internet for other guitars like Ben 2's. He found two… both well into five figures. He winced but what could he do? He had to have it. And it could just be the tip of a very expensive iceberg. Until the auction house posted the catalogue Ben wouldn't know how many other items he would *need* to own. He needed to start planning; work out a strategy.

Up early he made Gilly breakfast in bed, waking her with tea, toast and scrambled eggs. The smile that resulted would have warmed his heart at any point over the last twenty three years. He was no longer that man. His reason for her happiness was far more self-focussed.

He'd put her through a lot in the last week and, although he didn't care, he needed his status quo to remain. Her leaving him would be expensive, from hotel bills to solicitors' bills, both sides of which he would have to pay. He wasn't going to risk depleting the funds he needed for the auction.

As Gilly sipped at her tea, he suggested, 'Why don't we have a nice day out?'

'What about your private clients? Don't you have a lot to do?'

'I do. But I can do it tonight when we get back. I'm going to have to spend most of my time in the office for the foreseeable future catching up on work for Diamond from this week off. So I think we deserve a little *us* time before I go back.'

She smiled broadly. 'Sounds perfect. Where do you want to go?'

'I want this day to be about you, Gilly. Where would *you* like to go?'

He knew her choice before she said a word. She wasn't the most adventurous of people. She loved Stratford. She'd want to go to Stratford; go walking along the banks of the Avon, then lunch in their favourite little pub. He'd anticipated this, emailing a reservation before making breakfast. She didn't disappoint him by being original.

He smiled as she bit into the toast. She was buying this act. He moved his hand onto her thigh and ran it down the bare flesh. This woman had been all he wanted since they had met in sixth form; but no longer.

He would give her the best day he could, even take her on a rowing trip up and down the river, something they hadn't done in more than a decade, just not for the reason she'd think. He was going to make this a day she would remember because it might just stop her fretting.

Monday September 11th 2017, Solihull

Ben endured all the well-meaning questions on his return to the office – half an hour before getting near his desk. Even Old Man Diamond called to wish him well and welcome him back. From his villa in the south of France though, Ben noticed. He hadn't let it affect his normal routine a second time.

The other thing his boss hadn't let it affect was his work load. Kind words about looking after the Cookson account notwithstanding, Mr. Diamond had done precious little; buying Ben a week's more time to finish about all. All what Ben had expected and, if honest, what he preferred.

Having to unravel anything Mr. Diamond might have done was a nightmare scenario he could do without. With the tax man coming to audit the accounts he wanted to be sure it was done right; by him. He never enjoyed having to defend someone else's work.

Work was the last thing Ben wanted to be doing - finding it tiresome long before the last few days. But he needed it; or rather the money this would give him. Time to get to it: he called Robyn on reception and signalled he was on Do Not Disturb lock-down; catch up on the Cookson account.

She didn't question him. She knew the importance of the account and would only interrupt in the direst of emergencies. She'd probably think twice before knocking on his door if the building was on fire. He pulled his headphones from his briefcase and the CD-R of the new album Reuben had dropped off. If he had to work why not have a little musical accompaniment?

He reacquainted himself with the ledger, checking all was in order; whilst half-daydreaming of playing lead guitar in a rock band, in Domino Effect, singing these great songs, as good as anything on the first two albums. They were going to be huge.

Ben surprised himself. Concentrate on the work came natural; as it always had. He'd thought that part of his life past, but glad he could dredge it up when required; as he did now. Some things do never leave you. Two hours later he leant back in his chair and stretched out his shoulder muscles. The Cookson accounts were starting to take shape. It looked good. The audit should go smoothly. Good news; maybe if it went through with a minimum of fuss old man Diamond might dole out a bonus. It wouldn't be much but every penny increased his purchasing power.

He leant back in his chair and pictured that guitar again. The image of the Les Paul rarely left his mind these days. He'd had to own it; play the instrument his double had written all those great Domino Effect songs on.

Six weeks and he'd get his chance. Ben 2's girlfriend, junkie girlfriend as Reuben put it, had wanted the auction by month's end, but that had proved impossible as Reuben had suspected. It wouldn't even be in October. The auction house had announced November 1st with a viewing day on Halloween. Seven weeks and the guitar would be his.

Ben booked two days holiday as soon as the date was confirmed. Not a problem; few people took time off between the end of summer and the run in to Christmas so no worries about minimum staffing levels. The seven weeks didn't give him much time to prepare; they'd pass in an instant. He and Gilly had savings, most of which she knew nothing about, always abdicating responsibility for such matters to him.

Their savings accounts totalled a little over £75,000. Maybe enough for the guitar but what else might be in the auction he would need. There could be dozens of others essential purchases to be made. He needed to get his hands on more money, possibly a lot more.

Sunday October 15th 2017, Hockley Heath, Solihull

Life returned to normal; or so anyone outside of Ben's head thought. His colleagues believed it. Thankfully so did Gilly. Ben immersed himself in work, even managing to find a few more private clients. And he started to chase payment from the others earlier than before. He'd always quoted a sixty day payment period, rarely chasing before ninety. He changed it to thirty and started calling on forty-five. No one complained.

When one or two of his old clients had queried, all in a friendly way, all he'd had to do was mention Naomi's school fees and they'd even sympathised. People really will believe anything. It was going well. It raised his auction funds to £91,000; better but not enough. He needed more.

He looked at the screen, at the company annual return awaiting completion, but his heart wasn't in it. He glanced at the clock. In four hours the catalogue for the auction was being released online. In four hours he'd have an idea how much more he'd need. He felt nervous; more nervous than he had about anything in years.

The record finished, the clicking as the needle repeated its final circuit of the grooves restoring Ben's focus. He got up and crossed to the table holding the turntable. The clicking was a sound he hadn't realised he missed. Why hadn't he set his record deck up sooner?

Gilly had questioned it too when she saw him plugging all the wires in; just in a different way. With the record deck having been in its box since before they'd moved into this house, why now had he decided to set it up?

It was a good question; from her perspective anyway, one he could hardly give her the real answer. He half-mumbled something realising old albums didn't sound quite right on CD. Not a totally convincing reply but it satisfied Gilly, although probably because she didn't care. A fact confirmed seconds later when she started talking a Caribbean holiday come January; a chance to get away from the cold of the English winter.

It angered Ben, her talking about the Bahamas and Jamaica. One of the other women in her pottery class had gone on one the previous year, she said, and they'd had a fantastic time.

Well it might be okay for the woman in Gilly's pottery class. She came from a moneyed background. Most of Gilly's acquaintances were the same. Couldn't she understand that they didn't? They had to earn what they had; and by *they* read *him*.

Gilly was a spendthrift, spending far more than her little part time job brought in. It made him furious. How could she believe sponging off him as much as she did was reasonable? And now wanting an unnecessary Caribbean trip. Well he wasn't going to give in; not like he had for that Sardinia trip, or the Mediterranean cruise, or... He had better things to spend his money on.

~*~

The wait until 4pm had felt like eternity. It couldn't come quickly enough. But eventually it arrived. Ben closed the accounts he'd been working on and alt-tabbed to the auction house website. Nothing on the front page, but that didn't surprise him. Their website was appalling. The link would be buried. He went searching and a minute later he had it. He clicked the link and the pdf catalogue downloaded. His hand shook as he clicked it open.

His first impression was shock. It hadn't occurred to him that there would be so much stuff. He started to scroll down the file; page after page of clothing, video and concert props, records, books, and then guitar after guitar. How many lots were there? He hit print. He wanted to read this on paper not on a screen.

He pulled the first few pages from the tray, starting to read them as the printer continued whirring. There were items he'd never have thought he'd want. Even the mundane items suddenly became must-haves; Domino Effect guitar straps, wristbands, other ephemeral supplies. He could buy ones like them in any music shop, but having the embossed name on them made them different.

Then there were the outfits and props from the band's videos. Ben recognised some from repeated watching sessions on YouTube. These were an important part of Domino Effect's history. Ben needed to own them.

Ben started adding the lots up in his head. It soon became pricey. And this might be a best case scenario. What if the estimates were low? He needed to plan his spending. He opened Microsoft Excel and started to enter lots and estimates of the items he needed. Within a handful of pages he was over £20,000 and not listed any instruments yet.

It was getting worrying. How should he play this? He needed a strategy. The items on the first few pages might only be for tens or hundreds of pounds but they'd eat into his budget. If he bought too many he might not get chance to bid on the important lots later; especially that guitar. But… if he waited, keeping his money unused, there was no guarantee he wouldn't be outbid anyway.

The instruments started, with an Ovation twelve string balladeer acoustic guitar. Ben's running total already over £40,000 balladeer added another £500. The next two lots, both acoustic Fenders, upped it another thousand; halfway to his budget already. He didn't have enough.

How many guitars had Ben 2 owned? He seemed to own at least one of every make and model Ben could name. On the Fender list were Telecasters, Stratocasters, Jaguars, Mustangs and Jazzmasters; from Gibson SGs, Archtops, Explorers, Flying Vs and Firebirds; and Les Paul after Les Paul. It must be Ben 2's favourite guitar. Ben couldn't blame him. It was his favourite too.

But still he'd not seen *the* Les Paul; the one Ben had to have, the one in his dream. That would come later, in the really expensive lots.

Page after page it went on; Ibanez guitars followed Rickenbackers, BC Rich followed Gretsch. And then there were the makers Ben had not even heard of. Collings, Eastman, Grover Jackson and D'Angelico were all new to him. All beautiful, how many of them could he buy? He clicked the estimates into his spreadsheet, horrified at the total. If everything went for the minimum estimate the total was already £120,000; £200,000 if the upper. And it was getting worse.

Or maybe it wasn't. Turning the page the next thing Ben saw was a grand piano; £5,000-£10,000. Ben 2 was a guitarist not a pianist; the hated George Scott played keyboards. He could do without buying the piano; maybe.

With just three pages left Ben was shaking. The guitar might not be amongst the lots. He didn't even know if Ben 2 had still owned it when he died; if he ever did. He was convinced it was real, not just an invention of his dream, but as much as he wracked his brain, trying to think of where he'd seen it nothing came. None of the Domino Effect videos had Ben 2 playing a Les Paul. In each Ben 2 had been playing one of those tacky plastic looking guitars that seemed popular in the 1990s.

Had he been mistaken? Was it an invention of his dream? No, it was real; he just *knew*. He pulled the last pages from the printer tray and, relief flooding through him, there it was. He'd not been wrong. He released the breath he hadn't realised he'd been holding. Then he looked over at the estimate and everything changed; £60,000-£80,000, nearly his entire budget in one lot once you added buyer's commission. And there were two more items to come. But what could better that guitar.

The next lot took Ben by surprise. The first, Ben 2's motorbike seemed out of place. Rock stars owning a Harley Davidson always had them chopper style, like Peter Fonda's in Easy Rider. Ben 2 didn't. He owned a World War II military bike in original green paint. It jarred everything else Ben knew of his double. It didn't fit and he didn't want it. Good; that would save him some money.

One more page; what would be on it? Ben imagined another vehicle; maybe a car. That made sense. What the page held though when he turned it over did not. Ben 2's house was the final lot being auctioned. His house? Ben 2's junkie girlfriend selling the house he understood. It would make more than all the other lots put together. But at auction; not through a specialist estate agent? That didn't make sense.

Estimated in excess of half a million, it was way outside Ben's budget but it did give him one opportunity. Prospective buyers could go see what they were bidding on. A viewing was set for November 1st.

At the very least he could do that. He might even take Gilly; spin it as an opportunity to see how his double lived; how a rock star lived. She always liked that programme that went inside famous people's homes; the one with Loyd Grossman and David Frost all those years before. She would jump at the chance to see one in the flesh.

Saturday October 21st 2017, Long Marston, Stratford

The day of the video shoot arrived. Ben was torn between excitement and dread. Not a patch on his double in terms of ability, at least he was now a closer fit to him physically. His hair was longer than he usually kept it and he'd lost twenty pounds in a month and a half. His vintage Domino Effect tee shirt now fitted perfectly.

He pulled his car up outside the converted barn housing the sound stage. Five other vehicles were there already, all disappointingly normal; no rock star excess. It made sense. The band split without making them millions. Other than Ben 2 they'd returned to mundane lives.

He was nervous. He was about to meet Domino Effect, two of them anyway; George Scott still behind bars awaiting trial. Reuben had said they'd film around Scott's absence; easy to explain why they'd cut the video to exclude Ben Williamson's killer. It would even get a sympathy vote.

But it was the reaction of Ben 2's former bandmates that worried Ben. How would Thomas Paine and Lewis Alford react to him? The initial reactions of the other people who knew Ben 2 to how he looked hadn't gone so well. But Reuben had surely warned them what to expect. Maybe it would be okay.

Reuben greeted him at the door. 'Ben, good to see you. I was worried you might change your mind.'

'Why would you think that?' Ben asked.

'I...' Reuben started. 'Well...' That sentence too never went anywhere. In the end just shrugged. 'It doesn't matter. Come inside. I'll introduce you to Lew and Tom and you can all have a practice.'

'A practice? I thought we were miming to a pre-recorded track.'

'Well, yes, the video will be overdubbed with the recorded version but these things always work best if the band just plays.'

'But I've never played like this before. I don't know...'

'Relax, Ben. If it doesn't work we'll do it with the tape playing, but let's give it a go. You never know, you might get into it. You have been practicing the songs haven't you?'

'Well, yes.'

'I thought you might,' he chuckled. 'Come on, let's give it a go. I have a feeling you're going to be a natural.'

~*~

Paine and Alford were as uneasy at meeting him as Ben was meeting them. No surprise; he knew what he looked like after all. To them it must seem a ghost walked into the room. The greetings were hesitant; Lewis Alford staring at his hand several before accepting the handshake, as though trying to ascertain whether it was real.

It wasn't the same for Ben but he had his reasons to be nervous. As a teenager he'd played a handful of gigs in the pubs and clubs of Birmingham in the 1980s; to audiences you could count on your fingers. They'd been awful but the folly of youth prevented him from seeing the worst. At that age everything was an adventure. None of them had known better. Today though (he hoped) he was much more worldly-wise.

He took a deep breath, concentrating on one thought. People watching the video, when it was posted to the Domino Effect website, wouldn't know it wasn't Ben 2. Only the people in this room would know the truth. Logically he had nothing to fear. But logic wasn't always comforting. Rationality was overwhelmed by panic.

He realised in that instant why many rock stars drank – looking for the Dutch courage of legend in the bottom of a bottle. That option was denied him. He'd driven here. Warwickshire Police was far too sharp to risk driving drunk. He wouldn't have even if he could though. Ben 2 deserved his best, and there was no way he would be after several swallows of the whisky. No, he'd do this sober and to the best of his ability.

Conversation with the two remaining Domino Effect members proved difficult, the poor start of the introductions not being improved upon. Ben was grateful when Reuben interrupted, time to get dressed and prepared for the shoot.

Ben's stomach churned as he sat in the chair while the make-up artist and hair stylist, both male which Ben felt ashamed for being surprised at, were working on his look. It felt strange to have people preening him like this. It felt strange to be dressed as he was.

He glanced down at the ripped tee shirt and leather trousers the young lady had selected for him. The head movement caused the make-up guy to curse him. 'Fuck!' he said, voice thick with accent. 'Now you make do… fucking…' He switched to a language Ben didn't recognise, no doubt to insult him.

'Sorry…' Ben started to apologise.

'Silence!' He was ordered, then more of his native language; maybe Polish.

No one working this shoot today was English. 'Security,' Reuben had said. 'No idea about Domino Effect. They're not going to be able to freak out or head straight for the tabloids with an exclusive, are they?'

'Stop,' came a second order from the burly make-up artist. It brought Ben back to the now. The man was miming fidgeting. He was on the verge of apologising again but managed to hold it in. He didn't want more shouting; he was nervous enough. He stopped jiggling his leg though.

He looked at the man applying the make-up to his face. He was nothing like Ben would have imagined. If you'd asked Ben before today what a make-up artist would be like he'd have trotted out the stereotypes; very prissy women and extremely camp, gay men. The guy in front of him was anything but. Easily six inches taller than Ben and built like a rugby player, this man was scary. Ben didn't want to piss him off any more than he had already. He focussed every bit of his will on not moving a single muscle. Thankfully they were efficient and just few minutes later he was done; hair stylist too.

Reuben walked into the room. The look on his face shocked Ben. The man seemed appalled. 'Is it that bad, Mr. Reuben?' Ben asked.

'Bad?' Reuben replied, somewhat distracted, 'No Benny boy, it's far from bad. It's fucking spooky that's what it is.' He waved his arms enthusiastically. 'Come on. Get up. You need to see this. There's a full length over here.'

Ben lifted himself from the chair and joined Reuben by the large wall mirror. His jaw dropped; like the movie cliché. Spooky was a good word. Ben looked the dead spit of Ben 2 in full Domino Effect mode. He turned sideways to see a different view instantly glad he'd lost the weight; the tee shirt so tight his old paunch would've had nowhere to hide. What he saw eased his nerves; no one would recognise him dressed like this. Ben didn't himself.

~*~

Ben 2's bandmates had the same reaction. 'Holy Living Mother of Fuck,' Lewis Alford said when Ben walked out onto the sound stage. 'That's fucking uncanny.' Tommy Paine agreed.

Neither of them seemed all that willing to come too close though. Ben could understand it. They must feel like they're in the presence of some kind of ghost. If they heard me playing though, he thought, they'd know for sure I'm not him.

When the director announced they would start in five Reuben was nowhere to be seen. Ben thought this was unusual. He would have thought the man would want to keep an eye on all this – he had fronted up for the costs after all. Ben started to itemise all the individual items, estimating the amount Reuben would owe at the end of all this. Partway through he stopped. Quit thinking like an accountant, Ben admonished himself, you're here to play guitar – or at least to look like it.

At the one minute call Reuben re-appeared. Ben's mouth dropped open. Reuben was dressed like the rest of them. What the hell was going on? The others seemed nonchalant; as though his taking the place behind the keyboards was the most natural thing in the world.

Reuben noticed his surprise. 'Well, we couldn't spring Ben's killer for the shoot, could we?' he shrugged. 'Anyway, I've filled in for George on dozens of the reunion gigs. He was never the most reliable type.' As if to prove a point he held down a chord on the main keyboard. It sounded like thunder. Ben was sure he'd ever heard anything as loud before.

'Shall we get playing gentlemen?' Reuben asked. In reply Tommy Paine let fly on the drums hammering out a roll form one side of the kit to the other.

'Holy shit,' Ben said. 'They're all plugged in.'

'Of course they are, kid,' Reuben said. 'You can't play rock quietly.'

'But…'

'No buts Benny-boy; grab the guitar and let's get going.'

Ben looked behind him. A technician was holding out a plastic looking guitar– angled and freaky looking. Despite all logic Ben had hoped for the vintage Les Paul. It couldn't be here; it would be under lock and key with the rest of Ben 2's estate at the auction house awaiting the sale. Still he'd wanted it. This monstrosity was wrong.

The technician attached the radio pack to his back and stepped back. 'Give it try,' he said in broken English. Absentmindedly Ben held a chord and strummed. A loud crunching sound came from the speakers. Ben liked the sound but the tone wasn't quite right. Without thinking he reached over to one of the machine heads, twisted it slightly and played the chord again. Better.

Across the room the action received a nod of acknowledgment from Lewis on bass. 'So what should we start with?' he asked.

Tommy stood and leant over his drums. 'How about *Rock Me*?' he asked. 'We usually open with that?'

'Yeah, why not?' Lewis replied, starting into the thunderous bass opening. Tommy quickly added drums and Reuben keyboards. Instinctively Ben formed the first power chord of the song and awaited his cue.

When it came he was late, but only fractionally so –not disastrously. Ben was playing the riff and it sounded okay. He was astounded. Was he doing this? His mind told him he couldn't be and unfortunately his fingers believed it. He lost it and the song ground to a halt.

Ben 2's band mates were very understanding, reassuring him that all was okay. He took one or two deep breaths and tried again. The second time was worse than the first; as were the next four attempts. Ben began to doubt he could do this.

'Let's take a five minute break,' Reuben said. 'Can you all just give us the room?' He waited until the room was empty except for him and Ben. 'Look kid,' he said. 'What we've just done doesn't really matter. We don't need you to be able to nail these songs. If you just strike a few poses and mime to the tapes it'll be fine.'

'So why did you do it then?' Ben asked. 'Was it just to humiliate me?'

'Hey,' Reuben held both hands up. 'That was never our intention. It's just miming is fine but playing always looks so much better; even when put the studio recording over the film. We were hoping to get the best for Benny. But if it's easy we can just set the tapes going. We don't have to try playing.'

Ben breathed deep. He was being ridiculous. 'It's okay Mr. Reuben. I'd like to give it another try,' he said. 'But do you have a different guitar? This thing's hideous.'

Reuben laughed. 'Sure, kid. We have a few others. What would you like?'

'Do you have a Les Paul?' Ben asked.

'Les Paul, eh? You a purist?' He barked an instruction in the language Ben guessed was the technicians' native tongue. One of them scurried over with a red Les Paul, like the one in Ben's basement. Better.

Ben was warming up his fingers with Tommy and Lewis walked back in the room. His fingers were blurring over the fretboard. Tommy headed over. 'What you playing?' he asked. 'I can't hear it without it plugged in?'

'Oh it's nothing.'

'It didn't look like nothing. Your fingers were moving great. Plug in and play for us.'

Ben was a little embarrassed but didn't want to let these guys down. He fumbled for the jack lead hanging from his radio pack and plugged it into the guitar. The speakers let loose a horrendous metallic shriek.

'Fuck,' Reuben said. 'We must have forgotten to turn that off when we broke.'

'Sorry,' Ben said.

'Not your problem; don't sweat it,' Tommy said. 'Now play that again. I want to hear what you can do.'

Ben flexed his fingers and set them down on the fretboard. Slowly he started to pick out Flight of the Bumblebee, gradually increasing in speed until his fingers were a blur. When he finished and looked up three mouths were hanging open. For several seconds no one made a sound.

Lewis was the first to speak. 'What made you play that?'

'I don't know,' Ben replied. 'I guess I must have seen some kid play it on electric on YouTube. Why do you ask?'

'Benny used to warm up by playing that.'

~*~

Pulling out of the car park back on the road towards Solihull Ben was almost giddy. He'd had his fifteen

91

minutes, his brush with rock stardom and enjoyed it immensely; even if no one would ever know the truth of it. It had been magical. After his initial nerves and stuttering performance, everything had changed when he put the Les Paul around his neck. It was like it was meant to be.

He tapped the rhythm out on the dashboard as he hummed Domino Effect's new single. It was as good as anything he'd ever heard the band do. His double was a genius at song writing. Ben was happy he'd been able to do his part, little as it was, to bring Ben Williamson, the Ben of Domino Effect, and his music to a wider audience, even if it was in death.

Ben had enjoyed being with the band too. He would understand why Ben 2 had never lost touch with these guys after the split when their record label dropped them. Once over their initial unease they'd been great fun to hang out with. And to play with them had been a dream.

They'd practically gushed with compliments during and after the session. They enjoyed it that much. They wanted to do more in the future. Ben nodded but knew it could never happen. Reuben did too. Ben could see the regret in his eyes at the suggestions of gigging. It just wasn't possible. They'd realise it when their adrenaline dropped back to normal levels. They couldn't exactly go on the road with their dead singer/guitarist.

Even if they came clean about his not being that Ben Williamson, that story would be the highlight. No one would focus on the music. Conspiracy theories would abound about it being a publicity stunt; Ben 2's death being faked to get them back in the limelight. Ben 2 didn't deserve that.

More video shoots though appealed, and they were possible. Videos were undateable and could even include new songs. They had the basis of two from the jam that had just happened at the end of the shoot. That had been the most fun of all; the four of them messing around with blues scales. Almost like magic, structures had formed.

Lew suggested it could be the start of a lost album, billed as outtakes from the three albums. 'Domino Effect's Coda' was the way Reuben put it. And he would take the place of Ben 2 not only on the videos but also on the recordings and in the writing.

Ben couldn't believe it. Was this one of those moments you're supposed to pinch yourself to prove you're not dreaming? He had played guitar professionally. If only he could go back in time and tell his fifteen year old self all those hours of practice would someday be worth it – even if he could never tell anyone.

Then there was the not inconsequential matter of money. Ben hadn't done this for financial gain but the videos meant another £3,000 added to his pot. With the auction less than two weeks away it was a godsend.

Sunday October 22nd 2017, Hockley Heath, Solihull

Ben had the hangover of a lifetime – and all without a drop of alcohol the day before. This was the mother of all come downs. He'd never felt so drained. Even after the wildest university parties (not that he'd been to many) he'd never been so devoid of energy. But then again, he had been nineteen back then, not forty-nine.

He struggled to make small talk through breakfast; not that Gilly seemed to notice. As the days and weeks had passed since Ben 2's death, she'd settled back into her old self – narrow of focus in her views, outlook, observation and interest. He wondered why he'd ever married her.

Her self-absorption did have one benefit. She'd gone back to not caring about him spending so much time in his office. It meant he could plan his strategy for the auction.

He'd given up new work on his private clients' accounts. There was no point. It wouldn't bring in money in time for the auction. Chasing payments for work already completed was a different matter. He pulled up his client file and skimmed down the invoices. They owed more than £10,000. It would be unrealistic to think he could collect all of that in the time he had left, half the money was nowhere near due, but every penny could be critical.

Having hit send on the first email he stood and headed for the music system. The office was too silent. He knew what would perk him up. He watched the draw swallow the CD-R of Domino Effect upcoming album, then closed his eyes letting the music soak in through every pore. It was his kind of music. He'd been obsessed with Guns 'n Roses, Mötley Crüe and Blue Öyster Cult. How had he never noticed this band back in the day?

George Scott was rocking it on this track. Damn, he was good. Why did he have to do it? For money? It didn't make sense. The four of them had remained friends, close friends, after Domino Effect split. Friends should be able to resolve trivial arguments without resorting to violence; or murder.

Worse still, from what Tommy and Lew had told him, it was groundless. Ben 2 had turned up as usual with a bunch of demos; songs all done barring minimal arranging, something they had always done jamming in a studio. Ben 2 had offered arrangers credits for each of them on the album despite their contributions being minimal. But for some reason no one understood George wanted more.

Ben despised the very idea of George Scott. He'd destroyed the best thing in the world. But oddly he felt he owed him. Without the murder of his doppelganger Ben would never have heard of Domino Effect, not had this life changing experience. In a strange way Ben was grateful for the man's actions, He hated him all the more for that.

~*~

Ben was emailing the final reminders when Gilly opened his office door. It wasn't something she did often. If she was doing it now there was a reason. He muted the music.

'There's someone here to see you, Ben,' she said. 'He said his name was Reuben. Is he a client of yours? He looks a little shifty.'

Ben laughed. Her reaction didn't surprise him. She distrusted most new people. 'He might be. He was at the meeting I had yesterday.'

'Shall I bring him in?'

'No, don't worry. I'll go get him myself.' Ben locked his computer, stood and exited his office heading to the front door.

'Do you need me to get anything, Ben?' Gilly asked.

'No, don't worry yourself.' He was intrigued why Reuben might be here.

'Mr. Reuben,' he said when he re-opened the door. 'It's good to see you.' Ben stepped out of his house before Reuben could enter, and pulled the door closed behind him, feeling embarrassed by the normalcy of his home life. Reuben spent his life around rock stars and actors, all of whom no doubt far more interesting than him. 'Shall we take a walk?' had added indicating the path down to the field behind his house.

Reuben seemed nervous. He kept the conversation to prosaic items; the weather; the local football team, news headlines about HS2, of which it was obvious Reuben knew even less than Ben.

When they reach the fence separating the garden from the fields beyond, Ben stopped and turned to face his guest. 'Is there a problem?' he asked. Ben could see his hopes of an extra £3,000 for the auction fading. Had he put his trust in the wrong person? It wouldn't be the first time; he'd never been the best judge of character.

'No, Benny, no,' Reuben said. 'Far from it. In fact I have the money here.' He fished into a pocket and pulled out a wad of notes bound together with an elastic band.

Ben took the offered money and stared at it for a few seconds, trying to make sense of it. 'It's all there,' Reuben assured him. 'Count it if you want. I won't be offended.'

'Are you suggesting I shouldn't trust you?'

Reuben shrugged. 'No, I'm not saying that. A lot of people don't. I guess I just think everyone's like that.'

Ben stared at the man, full in the face and said in the calmest voice he could manage. 'No need. You wouldn't cheat me... Would you?' It had the desired effect. Reuben was a little intimidated. He broke Ben's eye contact.

'This isn't the main reason you're here is it, Mr. Reuben?'

'No, it isn't. Lew, Tommy and I had a long conversation after you left yesterday. They want to record that thing we jammed yesterday; have it as a bonus track on limited editions of the CD. It's too late for the sleeves; they've all been printed already. But we can add it after the final track – an Easter Egg for the fans to find.'

Ben's mouth dropped open.

Tuesday October 31st 2017, Warwick

Ben was pacing nervously. He glanced down at his watch; four minutes past ten. They were late and he didn't have time for them to be late. He had at most two hours to inspect the lots coming under the hammer tomorrow before he needed to be on the road. Reuben had booked the studio time to record the bonus track for the Domino Effect album on the same day as the viewing. Talk about bad timing.

He guessed it could have been worse. Ben didn't know what he would have done if Reuben booked the following day. What a choice that would have been – miss the auction or miss his chance to pay homage to his double.

There were one or two other people loitering in the vicinity. He was not the only one here wanting to look over a dead rock star's possessions. He pulled his collar up higher, hoping the combination of it and the beard he'd grown over the last two weeks would hide his resemblance to Ben 2. The kind of disturbance seeing a ghost might cause would get in the way. With the beard he was different enough. If anyone said anything now he'd just claim to be a relation and agree that they did have a certain likeness.

He rubbed his hands together. It was cold; colder than at any time since the previous winter. In the previous week the temperature had plummeted. He blew on them, eager to keep heat in his fingers. He needed them at their best today. Today his guitar playing was going to be recorded; still the most unreal of feelings.

At ten past thankfully the auction house finally seemed to be getting their act together. He saw movement from inside the building. The curtain covering the inside of the double doors moved aside. It was time. He began walking towards them. Six others moved forward with him. Six people who'd be bidding against him tomorrow.

It could have been worse. If Domino Effect had had the breaks they deserved there would've been hundreds. He remembered reading about the auction held after John Entwistle's death. The lots there went for ludicrous prices. Then again Entwistle hadn't had Ben Williamson's bad luck. He'd hit the heights cruelly denied Ben 2.

As the door opened he was first inside. He took a deep breath as he was forced to wait for the woman who'd opened the outer door to find the right key to unlock the inner door that led to the main hall. Couldn't she have made sure this was done ahead of time? Not in his time. He was annoyed; so annoyed he had to hold himself back from just barging past her when she did manage to get the door open. He managed it, barely; although more in fear such an action would see him barred from the auction that out of consideration for her. She deserved no such treatment for holding him up.

~*~

Ben couldn't believe how quickly his (almost) two hours viewing time had passed. He felt cheated. Worse, the room was packed. Nearly a hundred people had joined him viewing Ben 2's items; far more than the six at the start he'd foolishly thought would be his only opponents. Worse still he'd found out the auction was online too. There could be thousands of people trying to deny him the chance to own his namesake's possessions. He wasn't going to let them.

Halfway to the exit door he couldn't leave. He needed one final walkthrough. Although he glanced left and right at the lesser items and guitars displayed along the side walls there was only one he truly needed. He made a direct line for the vintage Les Paul. Two people were blocking his view. The nearest was reading each listing carefully, then jotting down notes in a notebook. Could he be serious completion?

Ben wasn't sure. Something seemed off. He was a small, unassuming sort of fellow. Fair hair, thinning; waist turning a little thicker as he advanced into middle age,

Ben imagined this was how others had seen saw him –
until recently, that is. He'd lost all his excess weight
these past two months and people were noticing the
effect his double was having on him from the grave. This
guy though had not had anything so transforming happen
to him. He was instantly forgettable.

Ben moved along to the guitar next to the vintage Les
Paul; a battered to hell Strat, Ben 2's workhorse by the
look of things. He leant forward and feigned reading the
auction card. His attention though was on the small
man's notebook. His manner was too methodical; far too
emotionless for your average rock fan.

He got his final clue when the man replaced the pen in
his pocket and started to move on to the next lot. In
doing so he presented Ben with a clear view of the
notebook and Ben recognised it in a heartbeat. The man
was writing his notes in a ledger.

He was an assessor; checking out the auction for Inland
Revenue. It made sense. The taxman would want his
share of the procedure of the estate sale; callous but true.
Ben knew how it worked. He had handled accounts for
dozens of estate sales. It had never bothered him in the
past. Each time he'd encountered wealthy families in
similar situations and heard their sob stories he'd always
felt contempt for them. It was almost as though they
believed they deserved special treatment; the kind
ordinary people would never get.

Today though, it was different. It wasn't that he felt his double's girlfriend deserved a break from the other inevitability of life. From Reuben's description of her, *Benny's junkie girlfriend*, and the tales he told, Ben wouldn't care if she never saw a single penny. In fact in many ways he'd prefer it. The money should be used to further the legacy of the man; not snorted up the nose of a dozy groupie.

It was just the mundaneness of the taxman and his approach to the task that bothered Ben. It felt almost tawdry. This small bureaucrat was reducing Ben Williamson's life to a series of ledger entries; a poor tribute to a life of creativity.

On the plus side Ben had one less competitor in the auction; silver linings. He tried to hang on to this positive thought as time ran out and he had to pull himself away. He needed to remain positive. This afternoon was to be his recording debut after all.

Wednesday November 1st 2017, Warwick

Ben had woken early. Like the previous day he'd left home at his normal time; having not told Gilly about the auction. He had no stomach for the kind of stupid questions she'd have asked, or worse moan about his wasting money; money she would insist should be saved for their daughter. She wouldn't even see the irony; considering her profligacy and lack of income stream had meant he had to work Sundays in addition to his full time job to fund Naomi's education.

The deception had had a downside though; the three hours between his normal leaving for work time of eight am and the opening of the door of the auction house for one final viewing session ahead of the auction. He glanced at his watch; ten thirty three. Twenty seven more minutes. He sipped his coffee and turned back to the front page of his auction catalogue; time to go over the plan again.

Ben had spent the past few evening marking the items with a code. The *must-haves* had an "A" written next to them. On the absolute *must-haves* this "A" had a circle round it. Next came the "B" and "B" circle lots, then "C" and "C" circle. Alongside each was a number; his max bid. Not the most complicated of codes he knew.

Anyone who saw it could crack it in an instant. He'd just have to keep his catalogue away from prying eyes.

'You going to the auction?' a voice said.

Ben opened his eyes. Next to him a pretty blonde waitress, no more than twenty years was waiting for his response. 'I am,' he said simply not wanting to start a conversation.

'I hear it's for some old rocker; can't say I ever heard of him. Was he any good?'

'He was brilliant; no one better.'

'Why wasn't he big like Madonna or Jackson then?'

Anger tried to take him over. He forced it back down. It was a reasonable question even if not too sensitively phrased. 'Bad luck. They came out at the wrong time.'

'Pity,' she said. It was obvious from her face she was already losing interest, which suited Ben fine. 'Can I get you anything else, Mister?'

'Just the bill please?' That got rid of her.

~*~

Ben took his place at the back of the room; choosing to stand rather than risk anyone glancing over his shoulder. It was the perfect position. He could keep the other bidders in his sight; watch them and learn their strategies so he could defeat them. It might be his first auction but he didn't want to give that impression unlike the eager beavers in the front two rows. A couple of them actually looked giddy.

They worried him. Ben had heard all about auction fever. Gilly had been addicted to antiques shows for years and he'd sat obligingly with her as she lapped it up. Still some of it was going to prove useful today. Not that he was going to thank her; she'd never know anything of this day and the lots he intended to own. They'd be safely delivered and stowed in the basement during one of her spa days. She would never know a thing.

The screen behind the rostrum flickered into life, showing Ben 2 in full 90s rock mode. The auctioneer climbed the stairs to the platform followed by a young woman carrying a laptop and a pile of papers. His assistant Ben guessed; there to handle the admin of the sale.

The auctioneer tapped on the microphone. Hearing nothing, he turned and signalled to the back room. After a few seconds he tried tapping again. When the speakers transmitted his tap to the room he settled in his chair and prepared to start.

'Good afternoon, ladies and gentlemen. Welcome to the Ben Williamson estate auction. We have a packed auction for you today comprising one hundred and sixty seven individual lots drawn from the collection of the late singer-guitarist of Domino Effect and composer of dozens of those annoyingly catchy jingles you hear on TV adverts.'

'The auction will be held in two parts. I am here for lots one through one hundred and fifteen. Then we will have a short break of fifteen minutes before my colleague Anthony will complete the sale with lots one hundred and sixteen through to one sixty seven.'

'So as we have a lot to get through let's get straight to it.' He glanced behind him as Ben 2's image morphed into a cardboard box full to the brim with stuff Ben couldn't easily identify. The auctioneer obliged with a description, 'Lot one is for eight Domino Effect guitar straps plus Ben Williamson monogrammed plectrums, wrist sweat bands, all unused I assure you, and other guitar related paraphernalia.'

He looked around the room. 'Can I start the bidding at fifty pounds? Fifty pounds anywhere?' Two of the hands in the front row shot up confirming Ben's suspicions. They were auction virgins. No one bids on the auctioneers opening gambit. He hoped they wouldn't have deep pockets. He didn't want these idiots causing him to overspend.

'Fifty pounds I have,' the auctioneer said. He turned to the second of the two eager idiots. 'Do I have sixty?' The second man nodded vigorously. 'Sixty I have. It's against you now, sir,' he said turning back to the first bidder who obligingly lifted his paddle again. 'Seventy pounds.'

Ben watched as the bids bounced back and forth to £110. Despite his determination to hold back for the big stuff it was difficult to hold back. He reminded himself what this lot contained; mass produced tie-in merchandise, not the real stuff. He had far more important targets. Still, it was hard.

The gavel hovered in the air; the auctioneer holding out as long as possible trying to elicit one more impulse bid. When it didn't come he slammed it down on the wooden rostrum, 'Sold for one hundred and ten pounds.' He turned to his assistant. 'Bidder 357, Ellie.'

'Lot 2 – a collection of vintage rock tee shirts three from Domino Effect, others featuring the Common Sense, Def Leppard, Iron Maiden, Led Zeppelin, Kiss and Van Halen; some signs of wear. Can I start the bidding at thirty pounds?'

The same two hands shot up; predictably. Ben hated their unrestrained excitement. It was degrading to Ben 2's memory. Worse they'd be taking his double's possession home with them and…he hated to think what they might do with them. Ben 2 didn't deserve such treatment.

The thought of them sullying these items was almost too much. He pulled a hand from his pocket and was on the verge of raising his paddle when his common sense prevailed. He breathed in deeply and kept his hand down.

The loser of the first auction eventually won the second for £95 after a back and forth in five pounds increments. Ben flicked through his catalogue. He had several more pages of pain to endure before the first coded letter appeared for lot seventeen – and that was only a "C". At the rate things were going Ben was going to have to endure maybe half an hour of agony watching lots he should own going to morons like these two before he could start. He wasn't sure he could last that long.

He half considered playing it totally cool, or at least trying to appear that way; head back to the viewing room until the auction got interesting. There screen in there would give him warning when things would get interesting. It would spare him this. Only he couldn't. He couldn't move. He was paralysed.

'Lot 3 is for a tour programme for the Common Sense signed by all members of that band; the final page of which features photographs of Domino Effect jamming with the Common Sense. Do I have twenty pounds?'

The same two bid. Ben cracked; he couldn't bear seeing them win a third time. This time when the bidding started to stall Ben raised a hand seconds later he'd won. 'Sold for ninety five pounds,' the auctioneer announced slamming his gavel down. 'Bidder 329, Ellie,' he added as Ben held up his bidding paddle. And that was just the start.

~*~

For all Ben's determination not to bid on small stuff by the time the auctioneer took a short break after lot 60, he'd won half the lots completed and his not-large-enough pot of money intended for the more choice items, i.e. the instruments, was depleted by more than £12,000. Worse than that, he'd attracted the attention every other bidder in the room; as well as the man holding the gavel. Every time bidding seemed to slow the man would look over to him. And the auctioneer knew his craft.

Raising an eyebrow in his direction or a quick comment of 'Are you sure you don't want this in your collection, sir?' and Ben's willpower was put to the test. More often than not it failed to resist. Ben's plan was in danger of being blown before it started. Damn that auctioneer. Damn him.

Ben closed his eyes and tried to calm his anger. He needed to get his focus back. Things were about to turn a lot more serious. Lot 61 was a guitar; the first of the auction, albeit only an acoustic. It wasn't a must-have though. Ben had only written a "C" next to it. It wasn't as significant as those to come. It hadn't featured in any of Domino Effect's videos, never been played on any of their recorded songs and there was no mention of it being used by Ben 2 to write any songs. Ben could let this go; keep his money for greater things. Or at least he could if his game plan was still in play. He hadn't been all that disciplined as of yet.

The auctioneer re-appeared. 'Thank you for your patience ladies and gentlemen. Shall we move onto lot 61?' If he expected a response he didn't wait for one. 'Lot 61, an acoustic guitar of unknown make; In fine order, plays well…I'm told. I'm not an expert.' He waited whilst one of the porters held up a tan guitar. 'Would anyone give me one hundred pounds?'

Ben gripped each arm with the opposite hand to keep them down and averted his gaze from the man he knew would be casting a glance his way. He needed to pace himself; keep thinking of what's to come.

'Eighty pounds then?' the auctioneer asked.

Oddly no hands were raised. Not even the two idiots of the first half. Ben scanned the room. They'd left. They weren't the only ones. The room definitely had fewer people in it than before the break. Maybe he'd scared them off.

'Fifty?' the auctioneer said. Ben kept his eyes away from him. 'Fifty pounds anyone?' Was there desperation in the man's voice?

A hand shoot up to Ben's left. He'd not seen this person bid before. Did that mean this man was only here for the instruments? Was he a threat, a player on the good stuff to come? There was no way of telling. Maybe he just wanted a cheap acoustic.

A second hand must have risen; the auctioneer announced, "Sixty pounds, thank you, sir". Ben located the second bidder just in time for the first to retaliate. Two further bids took the price to £90. How high were they going to go for a crap acoustic?

Less than a minute later he found out – £140; One hundred and forty pounds for a crap acoustic? No more; add on the buyer's commission and you're taking more like one hundred and sixty. Who would pay that much for…? Ben realised a danger was imminent. The gavel hadn't fallen. He looked down at his catalogue before the auctioneer couldn't catch his eye. He didn't want to test his resolve again so soon.

It worked. A few seconds later the inevitable 'Going once… going twice… gone,' was announced and the hammer fell. Ben had avoided wasting money on a second rate acoustic. It had been hard but he'd done it.

He repeated it for the next lot, another crap acoustic, but his willpower was all gone. Lot 62, the third acoustic of the sale, a better one he tried to reassure himself, was his for two hundred pounds. Lot 63 went the same way, for the same price; so much for determination. By the time the first half the auction was over Ben had bought twenty six guitars; only four of which had been on his "A" list. At least he'd managed to not bid on the pianos – it would be hard enough to hide this many guitars from Gilly, a piano would have been impossible. But even given this modicum of restraint his plan was shot to hell.

~*~

Ben spent the break trying to assess the damage of his profligacy. The plan was to spend no more than £10,000 by now; not be north of £47,000. His funds were depleted; severely depleted.

There was good news though. More bidders had headed for the exit at half time; whether small time players with budgets for just the cheaper lots or put off by his dominance thus far he didn't know. He hoped it was the latter as it meant his overspend might result in the lots remaining going for less than estimate. Even those still around might lose heart on lots he bid on.

Then again they might try to run him up, get him to overspend and use up all his money before the auction got to the best lots. If he was going to avoid that he needed a new plan and one look at the first lot gave him an idea. It was a grand piano. He hadn't bid on the upright pianos but a grand? They might think it his kind of lot. He could bid on it, only to drop it on one of them.

The new auctioneer, a much older man than first took his place and announced himself before lavishly describing the first of Ben 2's grand pianos. He'd done his homework, or someone working for him had. He detailed the songs Ben 2 had written or performed using this piano. Ben just wished he'd stop. He was making this harder to not want. 'Do I have ten thousand?'

Ben shot a hand up quickly, wanting to seem keen on owning it. It wasn't that far from the truth. His speed took the rest of the buyers by surprise. Ben might have bought nearly half of all the lots so far but he'd not done it impulsively, like the two overly excited idiots on the very first lots. He'd been deliberate, coming in as the last bidder each time. Hopefully they'd think he was losing his cool.

They recovered from their surprise and increased his opening bid. He replied each time and the piano very quickly reached £42,000. Ben took a deep breath and bid again, £43,000. Then he began to worry. Had he overdone it? Was the guy in the corner going to outsmart him and dump it the way he'd intended? Ben started to get worried; especially when the auctioneer announced, "Forty three thousand… going once.'

Fortunately his opponent in the bidding raised a hand, slowly. He was no doubt trying it look a pained decision; intended to make Ben bid just one more time for the *victory* at more than twice estimate. The plan was about to fail.

With a smile on his face Ben shook his head to the auctioneer and lowered his head. He heard the "Going once… going twice… gone" and the piano was sold. It had worked. The lot was over; £44,000, way too much for a piano. Hopefully one more opponent was out of the contest and maybe the others would be more cautious bidding against him now.

~*~

Whether his tactic worked, and the evidence was hardly in favour, it didn't affect the real issue at hand. Ten lots later, all electric guitars, all won by Ben, his budget was blown. And there were still the most prized auctions to come.

116

Ben was out of money. No point pussyfooting around it. It was true, plain and simple. But there was one thing in his favour; no one else knew. He had a choice to make whilst the auctioneer dealt with the next piano; one he had no intention to feign interest, knowing his trick wouldn't work again. Could he continue to bid? And spend money he didn't have?

Nothing would stop him; not today in any case. The buyers wouldn't know his budget was blown. He'd not given any indication of being worried about money so far so why should they think anything he would continue in the same vein. And the auctioneer wouldn't stop taking his bid. When he'd registered for this auction he'd placed £75,000 with the auction house; a kind of assurance to them that he was a serious buyer. They knew he had that much and so must believe he had far more.

He could continue bidding, win the lots he wanted and worry about paying for it all later. He was good with money; an accountant. He could work out the numbers out later. He'd find a way. By the time the auctioneer started detailed the next guitar, a Washburn signed by the four members of Domino Effect, he knew he had no choice but to continue.

~*~

'Now to the final three lots,' the auctioneer announced to the five potential buyers remaining in the room. Ben had seen off the rest. Good. Now it gets serious, he thought.

'Lot one hundred and sixty five… the late Mr. Williamson's most prized possession… a vintage 1959 Sunburst Les Paul.' He paused for effect. It took a moment for the words to sink in. He said 1959; not just vintage. Ben 2's guitar was a 1959 Les Paul; the Holy Grail. Now he knew no one else could be allowed to own it.

After a few moments the auctioneer continued, 'Yes, just this morning, long after our last chance to update either the catalogue or the website, we concluded our research on this and can confirm it as a 1959 Les Paul.' Another pause then, 'Can I start the bidding at £100,000?'

Ben looked around the room. No one was moving. They hadn't expected this. How could they? It made no sense. Okay for Ben 2 to have a vintage Les Paul, but not a 1959. Some of the greatest guitarists who've ever lived played their best on a 1959 Les Paul. There was no way Ben 2 had earned enough in Domino Effect to buy one; surely. But here it was; with a guaranteed provenance too.

Ben had to own it; no matter the consequences. He raised his hand. He kept it raised until he owned the guitar. He committed a further £305,000 he didn't have but it was worth it.

~*~

'Gentlemen, with the instruments now all sold, mostly to bidder 329, we move to our final two lots. The penultimate item for sale is Mr. Williamson's other pride and joy, his World War 2 military Harley-Davison WLA motorcycle and sidecar, lovingly restored to factory condition with all original parts, nothing refabricated, by Mr. Williamson himself.'

The image on the television screen behind him changed to show a video of the bicycle. The auctioneer let it run through the full thirty second loop before saying anything more. 'Can I start the bidding for this item at £50,000?'

'Thirty thousand?' a voice from Ben's left said. He turned to see the man who'd spoke. He'd not seen this man pay attention to any previous lot. In fact for much of the auction he'd not even been in the room. He was here for the bike purely as the bike, not its connection with Ben 2.

That gave Ben a problem. He'd been satisfied he didn't need the Harley. He couldn't ride a motorbike. It hadn't featured in any of Domino Effect's videos, nor in any promo material Ben had seen. Being a military vehicle, it didn't gel with the band's image. Had it been a standard Flathead with a bright red paint job and gleaming chrome it would have been different; fitting in perfectly, a two wheeled hot rod. But khaki green? No. So he'd been happy to let it go.

But seeing someone eager to purchase the Harley for a reason other than his double incensed Ben. And to let him underbid so outrageously? No. If he allowed that he was letting Ben 2 down. He raised a hand, 'forty thousand'. Out of the corner of his eye he saw the man who had tried to steal the bike with his too-low bid roll his eyes skywards. He gave up in an instant and turned for the door. Ben won the bike for £40,000. That showed him, he thought.

Ten minutes later he'd done the same with Ben's house; outbidding a man he guessed was a local estate agent. It pissed the guy off. He slammed his bidding paddle to the floor as he stormed out of the room, leaving on Ben, the auctioneer and his staff still remaining. Ben had won.

Thursday November 2nd 2017, Solihull

Ben sat at his desk at Diamond Associates glad he had a private office. He had the feeling he wouldn't be the best of company today. The come down form the auction was in full force. He'd not slept at all last night, unable to stop his mind spinning.

Ben looked at the level of financial devastation yesterday had wrought on his finances. He knew his budget had been blown. In truth he'd rather suspected he might get a little carried away. But there was carried away and there was *carried away*. And this was *"carried away"*.

His budget of around £250,000 was shot before he'd bought the Les Paul and the motorbike. But that wasn't the end of it. He'd bought Ben 2's house as well, for over eight hundred thousand with commission. He was short nearly one point two million with two weeks before it came due. Two weeks to find more than a million pounds or risk facing arrest and worse, losing all Ben's possessions. Time to get to work; thankfully he knew how to manipulate money.

He jotted the £262,000 he'd scraped together before the auction into a fresh Excel file. Opposite it entered the total purchase amount £1,432,493.90 then typed in a few formulae; shortfall £1,170,493.90. Wow, seeing it on the screen was unnerving. How could he lower that figure?

He had his long term investments. He'd lose a significant amount if he withdrew the money now but should still clear four hundred thousand, maybe more. He erred on the low side and entered £400,000 on the spreadsheet; shortfall £770,493.90. Under a million, that was better.

His house? Surely worth most of the remainder. He opened a listings website and searched for houses similar to his. There weren't many but if these prices were accurate he could get £600,000 for his. He added this to the spreadsheet; shortfall now £170,493.90, better still.

The problem though, was time. There was no way he'd complete a sale quickly; not in two weeks. And he'd not taken of the remaining mortgage on it. He still owed a hundred thousand. He felt his heart sink as he deleted the £600,000 and saw the shortfall jump back up.

Mortgage? Maybe that was the answer. He could re-mortgage his current house. That way he should get the money quickly. But he'd likely only get… what could he get on just his income? £300,000? He cursed Gilly. If she'd got off her arse and got a proper job...

No time for that. He entered the figure on the spreadsheet; shortfall £470,493.90. Less half a million but still way too much, especially given he had no more big cards to play. He was done for.

His mobile rang. It made him jump. He yelped at the noise. It was Reuben and good news. Reuben offered the possibility, no the promise, of further income. The Domino Effect CD had received enough advanced orders to make the top 40 – a first for the band. With the bonus track on the CD co-written and performed by him he would receive a royalty payment for it.

Then there was the video. It was getting airplay on MTV Rocks and Kerrang TV, entitling him to more royalty payments. And finally the last and biggest nugget; Reuben had sold the record company on a DVD/Blu-Ray release. One mention of the jam session the video was shot at and they wanted it for a 'Live in the Studio' release. All he had to do was meet up again, spend another day, maybe two, recording a bunch of Domino Effect songs plus a few selected cover versions and, maybe, some jams. It was a done deal if he wanted it. And he'd get an even share of the royalties; the rest of the band insisting on it.

The moneys he would receive from all the sales, airplays and other income this would generate would, according to Reuben, net him more he owed. It really was a dream; as though it was meant to be. The problem was timing. He couldn't wait for all this to filter through. He would have to get creative. And he had the perfect idea.

He'd agreed and ended the call before realising the dates Reuben had mentioned were in the middle of the Cookson audit. No mind; he had an idea for that too.

~*~

Ben was last in the office that day; not that it surprised anyone. He'd built a reputation over the years of being willing to go the extra mile so no one gave a second thought that he was still at his desk as they all filed out at day's end. They'd all think he was checking, cross-checking and rechecking the Cookson file; all typical of Ben Williamson the accountant.

The only problem was their logic was flawed. That Ben Williamson no longer existed. He was a different person now. His time in his double's place had shown him how things could be and he was not going back.

At quarter past six he did a quick tour of the offices making sure he had no company. The cleaning staff wouldn't be here for ninety minutes; time for the next part of his plan. He disabled the camera on the rear door, wiggling the dodgy wire Old Man Diamond had never got around to having fixed until the red light went out. The cleaners always left this door open whilst they went about their work as it gave them easy access to the bins out back. It would be his undetected way back inside.

Happy he'd thought of everything Ben left by the main door tapping in his security code and making sure he clearly featured in the view of the security camera and headed for his car and the shoulder bag full of a change of clothes he'd need.

The next part of his plan to work he would need to wait until the cleaners started their work. He needed someone to blame when the internal security system went down. A simple manual tripping of one of the office circuits, the one with the cameras attached and everyone would think a vacuum cleaner had overloaded it. Then he could retrieve Old Man Diamond's payment card and authorise the transfer. If Reuben came through on his end of the deal, and it was in his interest to, Ben could have the moneys back in place before anyone noticed.

Saturday November 25th 2017, Ullenhall, Warwickshire

As they entered Ullenhall Ben turned left, passed the Winged Spur pub, and back into countryside. Next to him Gilly was eager to know where they were going. She'd asked four or five times since he announced the day trip despite his saying the destination was a surprise and it was getting annoying. At least he wouldn't have to put up with it, or her, much longer.

A couple of minutes after leaving the village Ben pulled the car into the driveway leading to Ben 2's house; his house now – all paperwork having been completed.

'Isn't this that rock star's house? The other Ben Williamson?' Gilly asked. Ben didn't reply. He drove the car up and parked outside the front door. 'Aren't you afraid of someone finding us here?'

'No,' Ben said simply. Before she could ask anything more he pulled his keys from the ignition and was out of the car. He started towards the house.

'Where are you going?' Gilly asked. 'We could get in trouble.'

'Don't you miss those days when we would go on adventures, sneak around places we shouldn't be?' he asked.

'Of course I do, but that was thirty years ago when we were young and stupid. And People didn't have CCTV back then. Come back before they catch us.'

Ben spun on his heels; crunching gravel beneath his Cuban boots. 'No,' he replied and was round the side of the house.

Gilly hesitated for a second. She had no idea what to do. Ben waited out of sight wondering what her reaction might be. He leant against the side wall and lit a cigarette. She would disapprove of his return to smoking but he really didn't care.

He had time to smoke half the cigarette before Gilly plucked up the courage to join him. 'What the hell do you think you are doing?' she demanded. 'Take me home this instant.'

'Don't you want to go look inside?' he asked.

'No, I do not.'

'Well I do. In fact this second there is nothing I would prefer to do.' Gilly was looking petrified. Good, Ben thought. It was about time something shook up her cosy little world. He laughed.

'Take me home now, Ben.'

'Why? Don't you want to have a little fun first?'

'Ben, please. You're scaring me.'

He took two steps towards her. She flinched backwards away from him. 'Do you think I'm going to hurt you?' he asked.

'I don't know any more, Ben. You're different lately. I don't know what you might do?'

'For fuck's sake, Gilly. I came here to have a little fun and all you've done, since we arrived, is spoil it. Can't you just play along from time to time?'

She didn't reply. Even given the distance separating them Ben could see tears running down her cheeks. It was dull beyond belief; a stereotypical boring reaction. It wasn't even brightened up by mascara running down her cheeks. Gilly had long ago stopped wearing make-up. She no longer cared about making herself look good for him. Why should he care about her?

'Ben,' she sobbed. 'Take me home, please. I don't like you like this. I don't want to be with you when you're like this.'

'I'm glad you said that,' Ben replied. 'Because I've been sick of you for months, always whinging and crying.' He reached down and picked up a rock; his hand barely large enough to hold it. 'And I'm not going to put up with it for another second.'

Gilly's mouth dropped open, suddenly aware he intended to kill her. She froze; too scared to move. Before she could recover herself Ben was upon her, grabbing the back of her collar and forcing her to the ground.

She screamed. 'Ben, please don't hurt me.'

Ben just laughed. He brought the rock down, striking her left temple. It made a soft wet sound on impact. Gilly stopped struggling. Was she dead? He struck her three more times to make sure then stood admiring his work. It felt good seeing her like that. Why he hadn't done that years before he didn't know. He placed the rock on her chest and wiped the blood from his hands on her blouse.

He walked around the back of the house and retrieved the wheelbarrow. There was no sense wasting energy carrying her to the grave he'd dug yesterday amongst the trees at the bottom of the grounds.

~*~

Ben patted the earth down on his wife's grave, then raked leaves and stones across the bare soil. He wanted it to look as though the earth here was untouched; not that he expected anyone would ever look for her here.

He planned everything. It would take a forensic accountant to uncover his ownership of this property. He'd put everything he'd bought at the auction into a fake company and buried it several layers deep in government red tape.

He even had his alibi for his wife's disappearance sorted. He'd head to Scotland, for the Cookson audit tomorrow as planned. Gilly's laptop was in the boot of his car. The that he'd have two nights of husband/wife email conversations and MSN chats before Ali would discover the "*break-in*" at their Hockley Heath house Wednesday when she went to pick up Gilly for their lunch date.

The police would call Diamond Associates – Ali would know he was away and they'd confirm it. The hotel CCTV would back this up, logging his comings and goings since Sunday. When he heard of Gilly's disappearance Old Man Diamond would order him home on compassionate leave. He had his alibi for Gilly's disappearance and could make Domino Effect video shoot without anyone knowing. It was all perfect.

Ben walked back to the house. Outside the back door he stripped naked. The cold late November afternoon air caused goosebumps to rise on his skin. It was a small price to pay for freedom. He dropped the clothes into his newly purchased (in cash) brazier, poured paraffin over them and dropped a match in. Happy the fire had taken he headed inside to wash and dress. Within minutes the flames would destroy the evidence of his crime, just as the bleach would in the bathroom. Nothing could go wrong now.

He waited until it was dark before leaving for his and Gilly's old house. The darkness and deliberately broken light at the side of the house preventing anyone from seeing he was returning alone. He hoped it would be the last night he ever spent there. He wouldn't miss it. It was part of a life that was over.

Wednesday 29th November 2017, Edinburgh

The receptionist at Cookson's (he'd never caught her name) interrupted Ben and Old Man Diamond's meeting part way through his presentation – he couldn't have planned the timing any better. Both his boss and Cookson's CEO were playing into his plan perfectly, not holding back their annoyance at his having to be excused. How would that make them feel when he returned? He was going to enjoy this.

He walked with the receptionist to the private room where he could take the call, laughing and pulling faces with her about the annoyance their respective bosses had displayed. Time to start acting. It was Ben's moment to shine. He lifted the receiver to his ear with the grin still broad on his face knowing the woman was sneakily watching. She was that type.

He listened to the officer on the end of the phone announce herself. He was disappointed it wasn't DI Thomas, the woman who'd contacted him after Ben 2's murder. He'd wanted to be her; guess she won't get involved until there's an actual murder, not just a missing person.

When the officer got the part, finally, about Gilly's disappearance, he'd allowed his face to drop. A second or so later he pretended a stumble, catching himself on the desk in front of him before sliding down to the floor. He dropped the phone on the floor.

The receptionist was at his side in seconds. 'Are you okay?'

'My…my wife…' Ben stammered. 'She's…' He didn't say anything more. He didn't need to. This was enough to have tears welling up in the receptionist's eyes.

He heard the tinny echo of a voice from the phone handset and reached for it, still lying where he'd dropped it. The receptionist beat him to it and exchanged a few words he didn't bother listening to with the officer. By now her cheeks were wet. He was glad his performance had this effect. He'd practiced it in the mirror often enough. The receptionist muttered more words, to him this time. He nodded, not caring what he was agreeing to and she disappeared. Now for the next part.

Less than a minute later she was back, glass of water in hand. She lingered after he took it, resting a hand on his knee to show her support. He sipped the water, wishing he could celebrate with something stronger.

After a few minutes he'd said he needed to go back into the meeting. She'd tried to object but he'd said he needed to quickly pass everything over to his boss so he could head back to Solihull. After a promise to be as brief as he could be, she'd nodded and stepped back.

The two men looked angry with him for making them wait. That all changed when he told them of the call. They were now contrite. For the second time in just a few months he was being told to go home by Diamond. He should make a habit of that. Diamond even told him to just go – no handover.

Ben protested but Diamond, and Cookson's CEO, were standing firm. Family comes first; that old cliché. He'd agreed but insisted he stay long enough to prep Diamond for the last two days of the audit. To this Diamond agreed; even thanking him for his diligence in difficult circumstances.

An hour later he was driving out of Cookson's carpark – back to the hotel to gather his stuff and then hit the road. He should be back in Solihull by the evening, with maybe just one quick stop to dispose of his wife's laptop. It wouldn't do to have that with him when he got back.

With the other missing items around the house the police might even think his wife had just up and left him. They would question him but couldn't suspect his involvement. He was in Scotland when his wife vanished.

As he turned onto the M8, the opening chords of Rock Me blasted out of the car stereo. He sang along as always. He felt good about life. Even the inevitable motorway roadworks and queues would not dampen this mood. All he had to remember was stop not long before getting home and squirt lemon juice into his eyes. That should make them appear red enough to convince anyone he was distraught.

Monday December 11th 2017, Ullenhall, Warwickshire

Ben was sleeping peacefully when the phone woke him at five am, ending a wonderful dream. He was disappointed to leave it. It was his first uninterrupted night since Gilly's disappearance, Naomi having sleepless night after sleepless night after coming home from boarding school. Then Gilly's parents turned up the next day and for nearly two weeks he'd had to put up with all of them. Worse still he'd had to do it in his old house; to keep up the pretence.

Thankfully his in-laws noticed the effect it was having on Naomi and offered to take her away from it for a few days. He'd protested, again more acting, but relented. It really would be good for Naomi to be elsewhere. And he'd headed for his new home and peace. Until the phone rang.

'Hello,' he said, rubbing at his eyes. 'Who is it?'

'I know what you did.'

'What?' Ben said. He was instantly awake. 'Who is this?' he asked.

'Is that your first thought, Benny boy? Who is this? No protesting your innocence – just curious who might know.'

'Sorry, what?' Ben tried to sound as though sleep still had a grip on his awareness.

'You're not going to fool me, Benny. Don't even try. I know everything you did; everything. I even know where you buried her.' The voice on the other end of the phone began to sing the Teddy Bears' Picnic.

> If you go down to the woods today
> You're sure of a big surprise.

Ben didn't know what to say to that. He panicked and clicked the button to end the call; dropping the handset onto the bed. He expected it to ring back immediately. Isn't that the way it always seemed to happen? Or was that just in movies.

After a few seconds he picked up the handset again and dialled 1471. The voice read out the last call – made yesterday; Reuben, finalising details of a photo shoot. No calls since then; so who had he been talking to?

He must have been imagining it. After all how could anyone know? No one else had been there? He leapt out of bed needing to check Gilly's grave. Pulled a bathrobe round his shoulders he headed downstairs. He pushed his feet into his work boots, unlatched the back door and headed down the path to the copse of trees. He must look a site dressed as he was, but he didn't care. Anything more would have delayed him.

He followed the path by moonlight, not wanting to switch his torch on until he was well passed the treeline. As far as he knew no one had a view of this part of the property but why take the chance?

He reached the spot, the first time he'd been back here since that day. He'd not felt the need to repeatedly re-affirm his release from the tedious woman by continually revisiting her grave. It was enough to know she was here. He wasn't going to be that cliché, the killer who revisits the scene of their crime. They always got caught that way on TV.

His fears the grave had been disturbed were groundless. Everything was just as he'd left it. But something felt different? He couldn't place what it was. It was just different.

Then again, he guessed it should be. Time had passed since he buried Gilly. Rain had fallen. Winds had blown. Animals of all kinds had been through here. Any of them could have made the subtle small changes his panic was finding. The plain truth was no other human being had been here. So how could the caller have known?

The logical answer was they hadn't. They hadn't even existed. He had imagined it. Maybe it was the remnant of a particularly vivid dream. Maybe he was still dreaming? Could you have a dream in which you imagine yourself waking from another dream? A dream within a dream? That was line from some old poem, wasn't it? Ben couldn't remember for sure.

He shivered. All of a sudden he noticed the temperature. He was freezing. No great surprise; it was December and he was standing out here wearing only a bathrobe and boots. He headed back to the warmth of the house.

As he closed the door, he'd convinced himself he'd been dreaming. And that's when the phone rang again. He stared at it counting the rings; seven, eight, nine ten. After twenty rings he was convinced the person on the other end was not going to quit. Even so why hadn't the voicemail picked it up? Wasn't that supposed to cut in by now?

He reached out and lifted the phone from the bed where he'd left it? He let it ring several more times before pressing the button to answer the call. 'You went to look, didn't you Benny-Boy?' Ben dropped the phone.

Monday December 11th 2017, Solihull

Ben had no difficulty in convincing his colleagues he was feeling distraught. Since sleep had been non-existent since the call he knew he looked like hell; the bags under his eyes real, unlike the lemon-induced effect on his return from Scotland.

Walking through the door of Diamond Associates for the first time since Gilly's disappearance he'd had to run the gamut of hugs from his female colleagues for the second time in three months. He didn't think any of them had ever done that to him before Ben 2's death; now they were doing a repeat.

Releasing her embrace, Robyn told him Mr. Diamond was in and wanted to see him. Again? Ben thought. That's twice the old man had come in on a Monday, the only two in the last few years, and both because of him.

It went as Ben expected. 'Why are you here?' 'You should take more time.' 'We'll cover for you. Take as much time as you need.' Old Man Diamond was gushing when he sent Ben home.

Ben agreed, but hesitated, heading instead for his office. He couldn't face going home. Home was where the phone calls would find him; the phone calls that didn't get logged. Hopefully the voice wouldn't know to find him here. And he had to make sure everything was still good; that no one had uncovered his *transactions*, the ones that had paid for everything.

He opened the first of accounts he'd *amended*, seeing the problem instantly. The date on the file was wrong. It had been accessed while he was off. It was the same with the second file he checked; and the third. Ten minutes later he knew they'd all been accessed. But then, so had many others he'd not touched.

Had they noticed his handiwork? Perhaps not, he'd been meticulous, although he was growing less confident of his skills with each passing second. Panic gripped him. He couldn't stay here. They might find him. He grabbed his coat and case and was out of the door less than a minute later. They were on to him. He was convinced of it.

Wednesday December 27th 2017, Ullenhall, Warwickshire

Ben was amazed to be free three weeks after fleeing Diamond Associates. Every day, he'd expected the police to batter down the doors. But they hadn't. He must have down a better job of hiding Ben 2's house than he thought. Either that or in the run up to Christmas the police had been short staffed and moved him down their priority list. And it wasn't as though they would know he'd murdered his wife. They might still think Gilly had left him.

He'd contemplated fleeing the country but was sure the police had flagged his passport. He'd be arrested for sure making his way through security. That left just the option of going on the run in England. But that would have taken him away from Ben 2. He'd risked everything to get this house and the items inside it. If he had limited time he was determined to enjoy it.

His tormentor though, had other plans. Ben had unplugged the phone after those first two calls. But the phone would be plugged in and ringing every night at two am. Even after his taking scissors to the cord, it had rung; the cord having been patched. He'd thought of smashing the phone but concluded it would be pointless.

It would only be replaced. Someone was messing with his mind; breaking into his new home, trying to force him out. He wasn't going to let them.

The phone tormented him ceaselessly. Every moment that is except for when he was in Ben 2's recording studio. Even though there was a phone on the wall in the room it never rang. Ben had no idea why this room was left alone. It was as though it was special in some way; sacred. He didn't waste any effort on trying to understand it. He was just grateful for a place of respite.

He'd spent most of each day in the studio. Even without its current miraculous protective powers, it was a wonderful place to just be. He imagined his double would have spent hour after hour here composing all those wonderful tracks. Ben knew how he must have felt playing here. It was the first thing he'd done after the delivery van had returned all of his possessions to their rightful home. He'd unpacked the 1959 Les Paul, plugged it in and before he'd known it two hours had gone by. It was amazing. The acoustics were fantastic.

The house had come complete with the studio. His double's junkie girlfriend had been too impatient to arrange a separate sale. It wasn't as though she needed any more money. The first instalment had paid for the high of all highs. She'd never come down from that one. Ben saw the story on the TV, it being soon enough after Ben 2's murder that it was considered newsworthy.

No doubt his money would be passed on to another loser member of her loser family. With luck the funds he'd sequestered from Diamond's various clients could contribute to the elimination of a whole plethora of dope-heads.

Her need for that final, fatal fix had left him a studio that, if not fully state of the art, was everything he could need. Using it seemed instinctive. Perhaps he'd learned something along the way, picking up odd bits from here and there – TV shows featuring classic albums and the like. Whatever it was he just knew what all the buttons and levers and dials were for. A twist here, a slide there, a click somewhere else and the sound did what he wanted.

He'd started to record his own demos. He had no aspirations of grandeur. He didn't think he could take the place of his double. He wasn't doing it for any reason other than he thought it the right thing to do. Maybe his tormentor would to and leave him alone. Maybe he was a fan. He didn't think so.

~*~

As Ben finished recording his third demo of the day, the sanctuary of the recording studio was finally brought crashing down. The telephone rang. His tormentor had broken through whatever protective voodoo this place had. He picked up the phone. The voice on the other end sang to him once more.

> If you go down to the woods today
> You're sure of a big surprise.

Ben had hated that song as a child. He hated it all the more now.

'Happy Christmas, Benny,' the voice said. 'I have a present for you.'

'I don't want anything that you would have,' Ben spat out. 'Why can't you just fuck off and leave me alone?'

'But, Benny-Boy, why would I do that? We're just starting to become friends, you and I.'

'I believe you. Go away. You're not going to get anything from me. I have no money. Very soon I won't have anything. I'm a wanted man. You know the crimes I have committed.'

'True. You've done some seriously bad-shit, Benny-boy. But why would I want to turn you in? I have a vested interest in keeping you free. You could say we have a mutual interest in keeping Domino Effect's music alive.'

'So why are you tormenting me?'

'Benny, I'm not. I just want you to talk to me. You've not been ready until this moment.'

'And I'm ready now, am I?'

'You can answer that, can't you? You don't need me for that.'

'I guess so. So tell me what I need to do.'

'Well, Benny-boy. We're going on a little road trip, you and I. We're going to pay a little visit to Diamond Associates. We're going to sort out the mess you left.'

Wednesday December 27th 2017, Solihull

Solihull was a throng of activity. People were everywhere

'What do you expect?' the voice in his head asked. 'Christmas is over. Now it's time for the main event – the sales.'

'What should I do?' Ben asked.

'Just head over to Diamond's office. What you need is inside.'

'But how can I get in? They'll have deleted my pass code for sure. I'll only have three goes at guessing one of the others before the alarm goes off and notifies the police.'

'Ye of little faith. Did you think I wouldn't have Diamond's pass code? Give me a little credit.'

'How do you have that?' Ben asked.

'Please? Do you think I'm going to tell you everything? I might have your back but it doesn't mean I want you in on all my shit. Now just go over there and key in one-nine-seven-six-seven.'

Ben obeyed the voice in his head. He had nothing to lose now. If he was hearing voices he must have cracked under the stress. Could it get any worse?

Amazingly the door opened as the final key was pressed. Maybe there was something to this voice. Maybe it wasn't just him going nuts. Unless some tiny part of his subconscious had seen that code before and not let the main part of his brain know about it.

'Stop, trying to make sense of this and get inside,' the voice ordered. Ben shrugged and did as he was told. 'Now climb the stairs to the old man's office. What you need is inside there.'

Ben ran up the two flights of stairs to Diamond's top floor office. He didn't bother disabling the cameras today. There was no point; they would have captured his image the second he walked through the front door.

He hesitated before grasping the brass door knob. What lay inside for him? It couldn't be worse than the shit he'd already gotten himself into. He turned the knob and pushed the door inwards. What was beyond the threshold was something he would never have expected.

Old Man Diamond was at his desk. Ben would have wagered everything that the man would have been in his Mediterranean villa, enjoying the season. Why was he here?

'You!' Diamond exclaimed. 'You fucking ruined me, you shit. Have you come back to torment me some more?'

Ben noticed what he was holding in his right hand. It was a revolver; quite an old one. Ben remembered the old man had served in the army for many years before retraining as an accountant and joining his father's practice. This must be his service weapon.

Diamond noticed Ben's eye line. He followed it to his own hand. From the look on his face he must have forgotten he was holding it. The man's mind must have been wandering. Now he remembered it though, he was intent on using it.

He pointed it in Ben's direction. 'Get the fuck in here, Williamson. You're going to answer some questions.'

Ben thought about making a run for it. It was just two steps between him and the cover of the wall. Could he get there before the man could pull the trigger? Would Diamond hit him anyway? He was an old man now. How long would it be since he'd fired this gun in anger? Fifty years? Maybe he'd been a crap shot even then. No, he wasn't going to run. He was done backing down. He started to move forward; intending to jump the old man.

He didn't have a chance. Diamond might be old but his reflexes were sharp. He pulled the trigger before Ben had even made it one step closer. For a second or two Ben thought he'd been right about the man's aim. Even from this short distance – no more than eight feet separated them – it seemed the old man had missed. Then the stinging in his chest told him he was wrong.

He looked down at his tee shirt. It was becoming soaked with his blood. His brain supplied him with the most inopportune of thoughts. He was glad he'd not worn one of his Domino Effect tee shirts. It would have been ruined. He laughed. He was still laughing when he hit the floor.

Thursday December 28th 2017, Ullenhall, Warwickshire

Ben Williamson, Ben 2, was strumming his guitar trying to find the right chord sequence for the bridge in his new song. He'd been trying to find it for the past two hours but nothing seemed right. All his ideas had been good but nothing perfect enough. He'd got them all on tape anyway; who knows, one of them might fit into a future song.

He was just about to try again when the studio door flew open. Ingrid held her whisky glass in one hand, cigarette in the other. She was such a slob. If she wasn't such a good fuck he would have dumped her months ago.

'Babe, you gotta come fucking see this.'

'I'm working, Ingrid. Can it wait?'

'Don't be such a grouch, Benny. It'll only take a second.'

Ben 2 guessed it would be quicker to go see than try to argue. He replaced the 59 Flame Burst on its stand and pulled himself to his feet. If this was some kitten video she'd seen on fucking Facebook...

As he entered the living room, she unfroze the TV. She was watching the local news; weird for her. Then he saw what she was on about.

'You're dead, motherfucker,' she laughed.

'What the fuck?' he said. He perched down on the edge of the sofa and watched the report. The picture looked just like him and the name under the picture was his – Ben Williamson. He had a double.

He watched with rapt attention as the newscaster told the story. This Ben Williamson, the dead one, was an accountant, murdered by his boss after embezzling money from the firm's clients.

'Wait for the next bit. It gets even creepier.' She turned the volume up further. She always did like the TV loud. The newscast went to an outside broadcast. And it was truly fucking strange. His double had been killed in Solihull, on Drury Lane.

'Isn't that where your lawyer is?' Ingrid asked.

'My solicitor,' Ben 2 corrected for the hundredth time. Ingrid formed her fingers into a W for whatever, sticking her tongue out to complete the effect.

Ben 2 ignored it. 'I was there the other day. Man, that's spooky.'

The phone rang. Ingrid bounced across the sofa to reach it. As she answered it Ben 2 watched the remainder of the news report. Ingrid held her hand over the mouthpiece and said, 'It's Reuben. Do you want to take it?'

Reuben had been calling far too often of late for Ben 2's liking. Okay the man was good at his job and got the majority of Ben 2's bookings but far too needy; always needing to be reassured the new album was going well. Ben 2 nodded and held his hand out.

'Rube, what can I do for you?' he asked.

'Nothing, mate,' Reuben replied. 'I just saw the news and wanted to check it wasn't you. Have you seen it?'

'Yeah, Ingrid just got me to watch it. Fucking freaky, eh?'

'Beyond spooky, mate. I mean he not only looks like you but has the same name. Just glad it wasn't you.'

'You're glad your gravy train hasn't stopped rolling, you mean.'

'No mate, nothing like that. This is genuine concern,' Reuben laughed. 'And in any case I would have probably made more money cashing in on your death than this album of yours.'

'That's the cynical bastard agent I'm used to. You had me worried with the concern.'

'Well, I wouldn't want to disappoint. Now get back to the studio and finish the songs. We've got the studio booked for the fourth. You need to have it all ready. And for fuck's sake sort out your argument with George. He's pissed off you won't give him more than an arrangement credit on the album. You need to get that straightened out.'

'I will. Now leave me alone.' Ben 2 put the phone down and headed back to his studio. All thoughts of the song though were gone. He couldn't shift the image of his double on the TV.

He left the guitar where it lay and headed to his computer. Maybe there was more on there about the man who shared his face and name.

The End

Table of Contents